"*I just want you to know that I won't take this lying down.*"

"You don't have to take it at all," Max told her. "Consider yourself rehired."

Jane blinked, and Max could have sworn there were tears in her eyes. "But I thought—"

"I had. I mean, I did. Fire you, that is. But I've had time to reconsider, and now that I know who our resident astrologer, Greta Gamble, really is—*you*—"

"But you said that astrologers were quacks, snake-oil salesmen, phonies..."

Her voice had a certain charm, Max thought. Decidedly cultured, and almost...seductive.

"Don't let that bother you. Just because I'm not into it doesn't mean that our readership isn't." Running a hand through his hair, Max searched for the right words. It definitely wouldn't do to get this woman riled up again....

Dear Reader,

Welcome to Silhouette Romance—experience the magic of the wonderful world where two people fall in love. Meet heroines who will make you cheer for their happiness, and heroes (be they the boy next door or a handsome, mysterious stranger) who will win your heart. Silhouette Romance novels reflect the magic of love—sweeping you away with books that will make you laugh and cry, heartwarming, poignant stories that will move you time and time again.

In the next few months, we're publishing romances by many of your all-time favorites such as Diana Palmer, Brittany Young, Annette Broadrick and many others. Your response to these authors and other authors in Silhouette Romance has served as a touchstone for us, and we're pleased to bring you more books with Silhouette's distinctive medley of charm, wit and—above all—*romance*.

During 1991, we have many special events planned. Don't miss our WRITTEN IN THE STARS series. Each month in 1991, we're proud to present readers with a book that focuses on the hero—and his astrological sign.

I hope you'll enjoy this book and all of the stories to come. Come home to romance—Silhouette Romance—for always!

Sincerely,

Tara Gavin
Senior Editor

LYDIA LEE

Thank Your
Lucky Stars

Silhouette ❤ *Romance*

Published by Silhouette Books New York

America's Publisher of Contemporary Romance

Happy transits and many joyous solar returns to all my cosmic pals, with special thanks to Jane and Douglas Duncan, who are already on the Star Route; to Peggy and Michael Tims, who are celebrating their First Anniversary; and to Judy Grill, who is already in the Age of Aquarius!

SILHOUETTE BOOKS
300 E. 42nd St., New York, N.Y. 10017

THANK YOUR LUCKY STARS

ISBN: 0-373-08784-5

First Silhouette Books printing April 1991

Printed in the U.S.A.

Books by Lydia Lee

Silhouette Romance

Valentino's Pleasure #642
Thank Your Lucky Stars #784

LYDIA LEE

lives in an eighteenth-century country cottage near Richmond, Virginia, on property her family has owned for generations. La Bibliotheque, as the house has been called since her grandfather, a French scholar, wrote his acclaimed short stories there, is the perfect haven for her and her cat, D'Artagna. It was her lifetime dream to be both an actress and a published author. While pursuing these goals, she began an ongoing study of astrology and Oriental healing that she feels adds to and nicely balances her writing.

Her theatrical goal was achieved at the Dallas Theater Center where, as actress, playwright and designer, she received the coveted Greer Garson Theater Arts Award. In time, however, she discovered that only writing could fulfill her creative desires. When not spinning tales, she enjoys reading, traveling and the company of friends. Lydia describes herself as an incurable romantic who believes in dreams, magic and happy endings.

Dear Readers,

Ever since my mother told me (at the impressionable age of four) that I was a headstrong and dramatic Leo, I've been fascinated with the stars. That fascination no doubt propelled me into being, among other things, an amateur astrologer. As a writer, I've found it's been a real plus, since I've frequently used astrology to help in characterization.

In *Thank Your Lucky Stars* I went all the way and made my heroine an astrologer. Since the emphasis in the *Written in the Stars* books is on the hero, and since mine is an Aries, I've given my heroine carte blanche in decoding him! Needless to say, he is not interested in astrology, though he's definitely interested in our heroine. (When an Aries man sees a woman he wants, nothing will stop him.)

I think the *Written in the Stars* books are an enjoyable way to learn about how the stars influence that delightful dance we call love. Romance ruled by the stars? Who can say for sure?

Astrology is not an exact science, but then, neither is love. Both have fascinated mankind for centuries, but especially now, as we get ready for the twenty-first century, it seems that people everywhere are interested in delving a little deeper into the mystery and romance of life. I'm pleased that Silhouette Romance has inaugurated the *Written in the Stars* program, and I wish all of you many hours of reading pleasure.

Warmest regards,

Lydia Lee

Chapter One

"I don't think you've heard a thing I've said!"

The attractive redhead certainly knew how to stand her ground, Max thought. He was particularly fond of redheads. He'd read somewhere that Aries men went for them.

"I do hear you," he replied. "It's just that my head is not in the best condition, and if you'd lower your voice, we might—"

"Lower *my* voice! Are you giving stage directions or something?"

"I—"

"You fired me, and I want to know why." She took a deep breath and looked Max straight in the eye.

She had beautiful eyes. He'd noticed them last night, though he'd thought it was the effect of too much champagne on an empty stomach. Women named Jane Smith were supposed to be plain; wasn't that the expression, "Plain Jane"?

"I'm sorry...what?" he asked, trying to concentrate on what she was saying.

"I got this letter today." She waved the offending piece of paper in his face. "Something about overstock. What are we, dented cans of soup?"

"No."

"Then why did you fire me?"

"I didn't know I had." Maxwell Hunter took another deep breath and glanced at the letter she waved. He paused as the realization hit home. "*You're* Greta Gamble?"

"The same."

"But last night you were Jane Smith."

"I still am."

"Well, you could have told me so."

"Over the pâté and champagne?" She was pacing in front of his desk like a caged lioness, and the dangerous light that flashed in her eyes suggested possible mayhem. Abruptly she stopped and planted herself in front of him.

The champagne was dreadful. He'd had too much of it and not enough of the luscious redhead. Max's gaze quickly traveled her length. She was standing as straight as a tree, hands on her hips. Her black down coat hung open, affording a view of a maroon knit dress that hugged her gentle curves. Although she was tall and slim, he had the feeling there was a lot more than met the eye.

"And furthermore, astrology is a respected profession." She was obviously winding up a speech he'd missed.

"I never said it wasn't," he quickly stuck in. "Well, last night doesn't count. I'd had a bad day," He covered the awkward lie with what he hoped was a penetrating look. He couldn't remember every handling anyone or any situation this miserably. Never. And he wasn't about to start now, he decided firmly. "Miss Gamble—"

"Smith," she corrected with a toss of her red hair.

"Whatever your name is—"

"Jane Smith. We met last night. Remember? I had cut my knee on the broken light bulb."

She was smiling sweetly now, and Max noted that although her teeth were perfect, her mouth was a bit too large. Max liked a generous mouth. But, he reminded himself hastily, he'd seen women far more beautiful than Jane. Still, there was something about her.... The eyes; sure, it had to be the eyes, and of course, he'd never seen hair quite that shade of red. The color of cinnamon.

"Yes. I remember." Damn her cinnamon hair and amethyst eyes—she was confusing him!

"Well, really!" she countered, waving her notice. "I just want you to know I won't take this lying down."

"You don't have to take it at all." Rising abruptly, Max snatched the paper from her hands and tossed it into the trash basket by his desk. "Consider yourself re-hired."

"I am?" Jane blinked and Max could have sworn there were tears in her eyes. "But I thought—"

"I had. I mean, I did . . . fire you that is. But I've had time to reconsider, and now that I know who Greta Gamble really is . . ." Max paused. His head was beginning to pound.

"But you said that astrologers were quacks, snake-oil salesmen, phonies—"

"Don't let that bother you. Just because I'm not into it doesn't mean that our readership isn't."

"I'm confused." As if to prove her point, Jane sank into the chair opposite his desk and flashed her jewels in his direction.

Running a hand through his hair, Max searched for the right words. It definitely wouldn't do to get her riled up again. It certainly wouldn't do his headache any good, either.

"Miss . . . Smith—"

"You can call me Jane."

Now that her voice had lowered, it had a certain charm about it. Decidedly cultured, and almost seductive.

"Jane." Max thrust his hands into his pockets and stepping over to the window, tried to pull himself together. After all, he was a man's man—no false trappings, no excess baggage. And even though he'd been recently divorced, he'd had no need for therapy. At thirty-six, he considered himself fairly well adjusted, uncomplicated and, Lord forbid, not susceptible to astrology or astrologers. Greta . . . Jane was an employee at his father's newspaper—or rather, his newspaper, he reminded himself. Originally Max had agreed to come up for a month, help revive the dinosaur and then head back to the *Dallas Post*. His father's most recent asthma attack changed those plans. In the blink of an eye, the doctors gave the senior Mr. Hunter an ultimatum: either he step down and let his son take the reins, or be content running the *Heavenly Tribune*. They further suggested an extended vacation in a sunny, dry climate. Mrs. Hunter took this last nugget of advice, and before her husband knew what was happening, they were on their way to Arizona; and their son was the new editor-in-chief of *The Alexandrian*.

Max let out a sigh. He'd have to say something to the woman, preferably something mundane about her column. On second thought, that might not work; last night he'd blasted "Thank Your Lucky Stars" to Mars and back. Rufus, his friend and chief investigative reporter, had mentioned having Greta . . . Jane work with him on some reporting. Surely that was a safe subject.

Turning from the window, however, Max noticed that Jane, totally oblivious to him, had pulled out a steno pad and was scribbling furiously. She had discarded her coat, and with a tiny calculator propped on her lap, appeared to have made herself right at home. She was, Max had to admit, a vision. Soft morning sunlight haloed her fiery shoulder-length curls, and there was a blush of pink to her cheeks that gave her an almost angelic touch. Almost.

"Well, at least the moon's not void of course," she said, looking up at him.

"'Void of course'?" He'd been making a leisurely perusal of those long and lovely legs of hers and suddenly felt as though he'd been caught with his hand in the cookie jar.

"Astrology jargon." She tapped the steno pad with her pencil.

"You're rehired, Miss Gambler," Max snapped in an effort to pull himself together.

"Gamble. As in Black Jack. Of course, it's really Smith, but I prefer just plain Jane." Cocking her head to one side, she seemed amused by this phrase. "Though I'm still curious as to why you fired me."

"*The Alexandrian*'s been losing readers, advertisers and money. I intend on getting it all back—"

"By firing your staff?" She was smiling at him again.

Good Lord, could this be the same banshee that came flying into his office five minutes ago?

He frowned. "I was doing some updating. And at first glance, it seemed that, quite frankly, we could save money by using a syndicated astrologer."

"Undoubtedly you could," she murmured, returning her gaze to the numerous squiggles on her steno pad. "I'd certainly hate to bankrupt you."

"I'll try to remember that," Max replied somewhat absently, noting that Jane had just recrossed her legs for what must have been the fourth time. "However," he continued, "I can see that your local appeal is a real drawing card. And then, of course, Rufus mentioned your excellent investigative articles."

"Thanks. I look forward to doing more of them in the future."

Snapping the pad closed and uncrossing her legs yet another time, Jane rose with a grace that made Max want to reach out and touch her. Pretty crazy thought for nine o'clock in the morning, especially given the hectic day ahead of him. But there was something he liked about her. Still, all that business with the planets was ridiculous.

"There are more things under heaven and earth, Horatio...." Pausing at the door, Jane sent Max a smile that made him think she read minds as well as charts.

"Maybe Hamlet should have hired an astrologer," Max rejoined, determined not to let her have the last word.

Whatever was about to erupt from her delightful mouth was cut off as Rufus entered. As usual, he was dressed in the patched, professorial tweeds that had been his trademark at the University of Virginia fifteen years earlier. What was left of his sandy-brown hair was brushed behind his ears and just touched his collar. Aside from that, he looked much the same as he did when he and Max were fraternity brothers.

"That was quite a St. Patrick's Day party you gave last night," Jane said as she eased her way back toward Max's desk.

"Thanks. My grandfather always said that everyone's Irish on St. Patty's." He added, "You're sure your last name's not O'Bannon?"

"We've just been discussing Miss *Gamble's* various nom de plumes, Rufus."

His friend clearly ruffled, muttered, "Oh, yes...I see you found out."

"No real harm done," Max said with a generous sweep of his hand.

"Especially now that I've been rehired," Jane announced. "Oh, and by the way, my mother is an O'Hara." As if that explained everything, she promptly sat down and clutching her steno pad, looked expectantly from Rufus to Max.

Max, raising his eyebrows at this non sequitur, crossed to his desk. "Well, let's get down to business—"

"Wait a minute," Rufus interjected. "What's this about rehiring Jane?"

"It's nothing."

"It most certainly *is* something!" Jane declared, pointing to the waste-paper can. "Only it's in there. My walking papers. I got them this morning—"

"Your walking papers!" Rufus leaned over and retrieved the crumpled sheet.

"Oh, for the love of Pete! Put it back, Rufus. It was all a misunderstanding."

"Hey, you really did fire her." Rufus adjusted his glasses as if that might magically change the fact.

"Yes, and as she so adroitly informed you, I've re-hired her."

"But why?"

"Because...because we need an astrologer on the paper, that's why!"

"No, I mean why did you fire her?" Rufus was still inspecting the sheet of paper.

"Because he thought I was Greta Gamble," Jane offered, a slightly wicked smile on her lips. "And, of course, I am. But we've been through all of that so you really can toss that nasty piece of paper back in the can. Besides, I'm as eager to get down to business as you all are."

"I'm sure you don't need our help to write your column," Max said distractedly.

"Oh, but Mr. Hunter, after what you said last night—"

"Let's forget everything I said last night!"

She was doing it to him again, he thought. And by God, he was practically shouting.

"Everything?"

As Jane folded back her steno pad, Max wondered just what else he had said.

"I will *never* drink champagne again," he muttered.

"Oh? At the party you said it was the perfect wedding of the Irish and the French. Then when we got to talking about my Blue Gem, you said that one should never buy Japanese champagne or French cars."

"Evidently I had a great deal to say about champagne and you appear to have inscribed it all in your little notepad." With a moan, Max lowered his head into his hands.

"Don't be silly."

"Well, I'm glad you're still with us," Rufus managed to say. Unlatching his briefcase and removing some papers, he casually added, "I don't think the Japanese make champagne, but Max is right about French cars. I've been telling you for six months to trade your old French model in for a new car."

"I like my little Blue Gem," Jane said with a touch of stubbornness that Max found oddly appealing. "It runs beautifully." She held her pencil above the notepad as if she were truly about to take dictation. "Even though it's ten years old. But we're really not here to chat about my car. Rufus, tell Max what we talked about."

"Well, Max, it's about that astrology scam I discussed with you last night. If Jane here does get Dr. Zodiac to hire her—"

"Hold on!" Max said, "What do you mean *if* Dr. Zodiac hires her?"

"There's no reason to think he wouldn't. After all, he was willing to take her on six months ago." Sticking a pencil between his teeth, Rufus began to shuffle through some papers. "Ah, ha! Here we have Miss Devine's letter to the editor. She's the one who first filed suit against Astroscope, Inc., and—"

"She's willing to testify in court. Well, that is as soon as we get some proof and an inside scoop." Leaning forward as if she were about to be launched to her favorite star, Jane added, "Because if there's one thing that makes me see red, it's quack astrologers!"

"Whoa!" Max snapped. "I seemed to have missed something. When did you all hatch this plot?"

"Last night. It was after I cut my knee but before you returned with the champagne and pâté." Averting her gaze from Max, she took refuge in doodling on the pad. "And then when you got back, it just seemed better not to mix business with pleasure. After all, it was a party in your honor." She shot him an innocent look. "Even if you aren't Irish."

"That has nothing to do with anything." Max said, attempting to make sense of what he feared was a hopeless jumble. "The point is...the point is...I've read enough about this Astroscope scam to know they're a bunch of nuts and could even be dangerous. There's no telling what they're involved in. I'm sorry Jane, but this is one story you'll have to let Rufus handle alone."

"That's sexist!" Jane said as a rush of color infused her face. "I've covered several potentially dangerous stories for Rufus. Take the school-board embezzlement—"

"That was different. You were in the public eye the whole time, not holed up with some lunatic named Zodiax." Although his head was still aching, Max felt a little more in control.

"Mr. Hunter! What an un-American remark, or don't you remember the bit about innocent until proven guilty?" Despite her sarcasm, Max detected a devilish sparkle in her eyes.

"I'm not a lawyer, just a newspaperman. And in this case, the one who has the final say." He cracked a smile. "Call me a despot if you like. But believe it or not, I am concerned for your well-being—despite the horrendous things I may have said last night—and I'm sure Rufus agrees."

"Not entirely, Max. Maybe Jane should tell you about her interview with Dr. Z." Licking his thumbs, Rufus quickly rattled through more papers before retrieving another document. "You also might want to look at this flyer advertising his newsletter. It's hardly the work of a madman. Just a flimflam artist with slick PR."

Max rocked back in his chair. It was nine-thirty already, but he knew nothing would get done until he heard her out. "Okay, tell me about Zodiax."

"Zodiac," Jane corrected. "And there isn't that much to tell. I'd just come in from San Francisco and was camping out above a friend's grocery store on King Street. That was where I learned about Dr. Zodiac—"

"In a grocery store?" Max steepled his fingers before him. "Somehow I never imagined Buy-Rite as the hub of the occult."

"Not a regular grocery. The Happy Harvest Grocery. It's a health-food store that specializes in organic produce." At Max's grumbled assent, Jane continued. "Well, I saw his flyer—the same one Rufus has—and I have to admit I was taken in by it. I mean, who in their right mind doesn't want the good life? Dr. Z. says he can bring it all to you—for a price, of course. Well, at the time I wanted both the good life *and* a job, and preferably something in my field. You see I was getting a little tired of being a checker at the Happy Harvest.

"Anyway, to cut to the chase, Astroscope has quite a swank setup just off Washington Street down by the river. Imagine Art Deco gone mad—black lights, black velvet curtains, mirrors, black carpet and Italian marble." Jane paused, then on a laugh said, "Dr. Zodiac definitely believes in the good life, and after our interview, he was ready to hire me as a staff astrologer. In fact, unless I imagined it, I think he had other things in mind too. That was enough for me, or should I say too much!"

"It's out of the question," Max said, barely restraining himself from banging on the desk. He knew he was being a bit irrational, but it had been one hell of a morning. "You've been watching too many crime shows."

"That's not true!"

"Then I suppose you can blame it on Nancy Drew," Max rejoined, sending Jane a purposeful look.

Rufus, slipping the flyer onto Max's desk, said, "You might not want to buy used cars from this man, but he's not exactly an international terrorist, either. I don't think Jane will be in any real danger."

Max fingered the slick flyer. "He looks like he's doing a bad impersonation of Basil Rathbone. I wouldn't even buy retreads from him."

"Exactly!" Rufus slapped a slim newspaper in front of him. "And get this. It's their monthly newsletter."

"*The Purple Petal? Astrological and Psychical News of the Planet?* Where do these guys get off?" On a bark of laughter, Max rocked back in his chair, "And I quote, 'Ninety-year-old woman's cat leads her to buried treasure in her own backyard.... After only six months' consultation with world-renowned astrologer and psychic Dr. Zodiac, Jesse Flintridge communicates with her cat, Omega....'" Looking up at Jane, Max couldn't resist asking, "You weren't really taken in by this rag, were you?"

"No!" Amethyst sparks ignited in her eyes and Max knew he'd touched a nerve. So the impervious Miss Smith had a hole in her armor.

"But you *did* consider working for him—"

"Not after I met him. And I assure you, if I'd seen the *Purple Petal,* I wouldn't have bothered."

"Well, that's some relief," Max said as he skimmed another article. Then, slowly looking up, he added, "For ninety-five dollars a year, you can not only subscribe to this font of wisdom, but you will be under the protection of Zodiac himself. Kind of like health insurance.''

"Listen Max, if I can infiltrate—''

"There you go again, talking like—''

"Not Nancy Drew *or Police Woman.*'' Clasping her notepad to her chest, Jane leaned forward. "I'm talking like myself. Look, I've got the credentials. Zodiac will hire me. I'll get the story—maybe even some proof to corroborate Miss Devine's allegations—and write a piece that will make page one of *The Alexandrian.* Maybe double your subscribers. That's what you want, isn't it?''

"You're pretty well informed," Max noted crisply.

"Jane and I have been in consultation on this," Rufus interjected.

"So I was told. However, I'm still holding my ground—''

"I see. No doubt you would prefer posing as an astrologer and doing the story yourself?'' Jane tossed back. "You know, you're acting just like an Aries with—''

"And what's that supposed to mean?''

"You didn't let me finish. An Aries with a Taurus moon. A macho, fiery, stubborn Ram.'' She smiled like a cat who'd just dined on canary. "When *were* you born? And where?''

Max looked skeptically from her notepad to her calculator. "April 4. Washington, D.C.'' For some bizarre reason, he felt as if she'd just extracted top-secret information.

"Year?'' She didn't even bother to look up.

"Nineteen fifty— Look, this is ridiculous. I don't even believe in this nonsense—''

"Nineteen Fifty?" This time she looked up. "So, you're going to be forty-one..." Diligently she punched this into her calculator.

"Fifty-four," Rufus corrected.

"Fifty-four years old?" Jane's head snapped up.

"No, he means I was born in 1954!" Max shot to his feet and planting both hands on his desk, leaned toward Jane. "I think this is all tommy rot!"

"I know. That's obviously why you lied about your age. You were trying to disprove astrology, weren't you?" As she leveled her eyes at Max, he felt all the resolve go out of him.

"I am not trying to do anything, except have the meeting with Rufus as planned!"

"Shh. I can't concentrate when you're yelling at me." Returning her gaze to the calculator, she said, "It's amazing how quickly this little gadget works.... Ah, just as I thought. Moon in Taurus *and* conjunct Venus." After chewing on her pencil for a moment, she muttered, "Oh dear, New Year's was kind of tricky, wasn't it? Some sort of deception involved with your work, and I'd say several illusions got shattered."

"I found out Santa Claus lives in Hawaii instead of the North Pole!"

"Well, you don't have to get testy about it. You know, if I were you—"

"Well, you aren't." Damn, what was it with this woman?

"*If* I were you, I'd slow down a little or Uranus will make tread marks across you." Snapping her calculator closed, she rose to her feet. "I don't suppose you know what time you were born, do you?"

"Six a.m. Satisfied?"

"Time out! Time out," Rufus boomed. "I'm a Taurus and I've just about had it. You two can continue this another time, but I've got a job to do."

"Well, if it involves Dr. Zodiac, count me in. Because in spite of what he thinks, I'm in on this!" With a cheery wave, Jane headed toward the door.

"You have a column to write," Max called after her.

"What would I do without you to remind me?" she parried. "Oh, thanks for rehiring me."

"It was nothing," he shouted, "Nothing but a lapse in my sanity."

Jane spun around at the door, "It's just Uranus and Neptune playing havoc with your Sun."

"I don't care what the blasted planets are doing! I'm running a newspaper, not an astrology service." With the back of his hand, Max whacked the copy of *The Purple Petal,* and proudly added, "A newspaper, you know?"

"Oh, yes ... The headline on that issue features Jesse Flintridge and her cat Omega, I believe. Top-rate reporting!" Without waiting for Max's reaction, Jane scooted down the broad hall to the sanctity of her airy office.

Although it was never as neat as she would have liked, it was her haven and as such, was packed with the necessities of life: namely a set of glassed-in bookcases, a homemade desk consisting of a six-foot door propped on two mismatched file cabinets and several hanging plants that flourished in the bay window and seemed to require very little water. Tacked above her computer were several star charts and an astrological calendar. It was a cozy office.

Pausing in the doorway, Jane surveyed the various stacks of books and papers that surrounded her desk like land mines. Every few days she would attempt to stuff them into bookshelves and cabinets, but ended up simply rearranging them into neater, smaller piles.

"And I have my job!" she sang out to the plants. Then, tossing her notepad onto the desk and dropping her purse to the floor, she collapsed onto her swivel chair and stared at the computer's blank screen.

Maxwell Cornelius Hunter III. Even saying that absurdly long name gave her goose bumps. Being in the same room with him wreaked havoc with every sane thought she had. It made her knees go to jelly, something she thought only happened in books, and sent her heart on the Boston Marathon. So, why on earth did she bring out the big guns as if he were the armada? Trying to convince herself it was because he had fired her didn't work. Last night, when she was just plain Jane Smith and they were drinking champagne, she'd felt as if she were on a rocket to the Milky Way. Even his barbs about astrologers hadn't phased her.

Well, not too much. Jane leaned forward and flicked on the computer, then waited a split second before loading her program. If only she hadn't been eavesdropping; if only she hadn't knocked over that brass lamp; if only Max wasn't Max. Pushing these thoughts aside, Jane entered the date, March 18. The day after St. Patrick's Day.

St. Patrick's Day. Lord, would she ever forget it? Still, she had to admit that despite the mishap with the lamp and Max's little astrology bash, it had been a great party. She and Rufus had gone wild with the decorations: green streamers, green balloons and bowls of green carnations. Rufus's Federal-style house, not far from Jane's, in the heart of Old Town Alexandria was the perfect setting for the festivities....

Jane, having arrived early to help with last-minute details, was putting her coat in an upstairs bedroom when she heard Rufus talking to someone in the adjoining room. Whoever that someone was had a voice that stopped her in her tracks; it was deep and rich and sent little shivers up her spine. Crouching down, Jane shamelessly listened at the door.

"Astrodynamics, Inc.? Don't tell me—it's a self-help movement, right?"

"Close. But it's called Astroscope, and if Miss Devine's allegations are correct, it's an astrology scam. Although Dr. Z. doesn't know it, she plans on taking him to court with a claim that Astroscope uses illegal means to terrorize their clients."

"Terrorize? Isn't that a little bit strong?"

"Those are her words, old boy. Besides, you know how theatrical people exaggerate."

"Does she have proof?"

"That part's hazy," Rufus replied. "But I figure that's where we come in. It would be a great scoop for *The Alexandrian*. In fact, I've got an associate I want you to meet who'd be perfect for undercover."

"This is a newspaper, not the FBI."

At Rufus's muffled reply, Jane inched forward, which was no easy trick in sling-back heels and a sequined dress. She knew that she was the associate he referred to—they'd already discussed the story—and the person to whom he was speaking would have to be Max Hunter, their new boss. Too bad she had been on vacation when he'd arrived from Dallas, she thought, but perhaps meeting him on St. Patrick's Day would bring her luck at the paper. Pressing her ear practically to the wall, Jane strained to hear more, then rocking back on her heels, she realized how ridiculous she looked. She had definitely been reading too many mysteries. She also had a cramp in her leg.

In the next room, Max had raised his voice. "Well, I say that anyone with a brain would toss off astrology as bunk!"

"Lots of people take it seriously."

"Idiots, maybe. And speaking of which— Hey what was that?"

Jane knew. It was a brass lamp, the one she'd just knocked over when she'd staggered to her feet in an attempt to ease the cramp in her leg. The reverberating clang filled the air like a summons to a temple. Oh, Lord, she really was an idiot! At least the cramp had subsided, but as Jane knelt to retrieve the lamp, her knee met with the broken light bulb and she let out a yelp.

"Who's in here?" Rufus demanded as he rushed into the darkened bedroom. Light from the hall spilled onto Jane, who was muttering curses under her breath.

"It's just me," she snapped, thoroughly irritated at her own clumsiness. As an overhead light flashed on, she squinted in Rufus's direction, but when she saw the man at his side, she took a deep breath. He had to be Robert Redford's twin brother. For a moment, Jane forgot her firm resolve not to get involved with another blond charmer. She even forgot she was sprawled on Rufus's nice wall-to-wall carpet with bloody knees. She might even have forgotten her name, except that Rufus, thoroughly alarmed, called it out.

"Jane! What on earth happened to you?"

"I fell." Jane looked from Rufus to Robert Redford. He was tall, probably six-three to her five-nine. And though he wore his dinner jacket with a casual air, she couldn't help but notice the rippling outline of his shoulders as they strained against the fabric. When he crouched down beside her, her heart went into over-drive. Rufus said something about getting some hydrogen peroxide, then tossing introductions over his shoulder, left the room.

"The cut's not that bad," Jane heard herself say as she gingerly pushed aside a shred of green stocking and removed the sliver of light bulb from her knee.

"Maybe I could help you onto the bed," Max said in a voice that suggested absolutely nothing ruffled him.

One arm easily swept around her, and before she knew what had happened, they had both landed, rather ignominiously, on the edge of Rufus's waterbed, only to flop back onto it in a burst of laughter.

"Thanks," Jane managed to say as they struggled to a sitting position. His arm was still around her, and even though there was something wonderful about that, it was also scary.

He had that drop-dead magnetism, the kind *Cosmopolitan* warned its readers not to take too seriously. But at that moment, warnings were the last thing Jane wanted to think about. Besides, the way he zeroed in on her with those cobalt-blue eyes, she felt as if all rational thought had abandoned her. She'd never seen eyes quite that shade before. And as he leaned closer, she could detect a faint smell of wood smoke...and something else—something very primal and arousing. It was then she knew she was in trouble with a capital *T.*

But that was last night, and this morning was this morning. Who did he think he was anyway, to tell her she couldn't take on Dr. Z.? Jane's fingers flew across the computer keyboard, but her mind was clearly not on the day's column. Max had probably been told he looked like Redford so often that he thought he was!

Typical of Aries, it had gone to his head. So he was handsome. So was her ex-boyfriend, although unlike Max's rough and tumble looks, he'd been sort of a surfboard blond. But Jane certainly didn't need to think about him.

Propping her elbows on the desk Jane forced her attention back to her column.

Moon and Venus coupled in earthy Taurus, promise lots of hugs. Watch out Earthlings, the closing opposition to Pluto could be explosive...

Damn! Usually it flowed right out of her. Today was obviously different. Swiveling toward her phone, she picked up the receiver, looked up a number, punched it in and patiently waited.

"Good morning," she said in honeyed tones. "I'd like to speak with Dr. Zodiac. Tell him it's Amber Starr.... Yes, I'll wait." Pushing away from the desk, and looking up, she saw Max leaning pensively against the doorjamb. A disturbing smile kindled in his eyes.

"Amber Starr? Just how many aliases do you have, Miss Gamble?"

Chapter Two

The look on Jane's face was supposed to make Max feel guilty. Just why, he couldn't say. He did not, however, feel one shred of guilt. He'd come bearing the olive branch, while she was planning mutiny behind his back. So much for magnanimous gestures.

"When you have time, Ms....*Starr,* I'd like a word with you." Instead of leaving, Max ignored the fact that she was still on the phone and sauntered into her office, pointedly keeping his back to her. As he surveyed the haphazard decor, he rethought his strategies.

The woman was definitely the type who loved to complicate things. This phone call to Dr. Z. was the perfect example. Here Max had decided to give her the job, after all, send her into the den of *The Purple Petal,* but could she wait? No. Nancy Drew had to do things her way. Absently Max's gaze landed on a stack of books precariously resting on the edge of her desk: Agatha Christie, Sir Arthur Conan Doyle, and...his eyes strained to read the third volume. Carolyn Keene? Who the devil was Carolyn Keene? Undoubtedly another mystery author, Max thought as he inspected the faded blue volume. Being a Sherlock Holmes addict, he could hardly fault her. Still, he was right, she *did* think she was... *The Mystery of Larkspur Lane?*

With a laugh, he opened the book and pivoting on his heels, turned to Jane.

"Nancy Drew!"

"That's a gift for my niece," she said, cupping her hand over the receiver's mouthpiece.

"Naturally," he murmured, flipping several pages. "'This is the property of Jane O'Hara— Hands off! 1948'?" With a grin, Max gently deposited the book back on her desk.

"It was my mother's—" Abruptly Jane swiveled away from him and spoke into the phone. "No, it would be better if I called Dr. Zodiac back. Just leave the message that Amber Starr will be getting in touch with him about the job offer."

"You're pretty sure about that position, aren't you?" Max purred as she hung up. "Oh, and that was a smart move not giving out *The Alexandrian*'s number. But then, you're fairly well versed in these matters." He tapped the stack of books, then settling into a chair opposite her, said, "I should be angry with you, but since that doesn't seem to get us anywhere, I've come with a proposition. Interested in hearing about it over lunch?"

"Lunch...?" She said the word as if she'd never heard of it before.

"Yes. A quaint custom where people take a break and put food into their mouths. My treat."

"I know what you mean," she said with a peevish shrug. "I simply thought that after... Well, you know, after—"

"The phone call to Dr. Zodiax?"

"Zodiac," she corrected with a laugh.

"The same. And we'll discuss that, too...over lunch."

"Well, I'm glad to see you don't harbor hard feelings. But then Aries rarely do." The full-blown smile that danced on her lips sent an unexpected coil of heat through him.

"You'll have to tell me more about Aries."

"That tomfoolery?"

"I'm not saying I'm a convert, just curious." That wasn't all he was curious about, he thought as he passed an appreciative look over her.

"Thanks for the lunch invite, but I'm tied up. Perhaps tomorrow. Or we could meet this afternoon. Who knows, maybe I'll have heard from our friend at Astroscope by then."

"Let's make it dinner," Max said abruptly. "You name the restaurant." He'd have to think of something fast to keep her busy while he did some preliminary inquiries into Astroscope. "In the meantime," he added, rising to his feet, "since you're determined to investigate Dr. Z., give that Sherry Devine a call and set up an interview with her." Withdrawing a card from his breast pocket, he snapped it down on *The Mystery of Larkspur Lane*. "Here's her number. Go for the personal angle."

"Max Hunter, if you think that dragging a red herring across the trail is going to—"

"I don't know what you're talking about," Max glibly lied.

"Oh, yes, you do." As Jane pushed herself out of her chair, Max couldn't help but admire her directness *and* the statuesque way she had of carrying herself. "You're planning on sending me on a wild-goose chase."

"I've never heard Sherry Devine called a 'wild goose' before!"

"Topless dancer—same difference," Jane snapped back.

"I believe she bills herself as an 'exotic dancer,' and there's no mention of geese, wild or domesticated. Now, get going!"

"I'll think about it." She gave a toss of her curls, then snatched up the card. "The Golden Garter? Oh, please."

"Maybe you'd like to go there for dinner. I believe Monday is ladies' night." Throwing his hands up in mock defence, Max edged toward the door.

"Why don't *you* cover Sherry Devine?"

"What an interesting proposition."

"I'm sure Miss Devine would be more than willing." Narrowing her eyes, Jane added, "Maxwell Hunter, you're very stubborn."

"Oh, is that an Aries trait?"

"No. That's a Taurus moon trait."

"And where might your moon be?"

"Taurus! So don't wave any more red flags in front of me!" Turning toward the ringing phone, she yanked it out of its cradle, then hearing her friend Hannah's voice, took a deep breath and slowly sank into her chair.

"Hold on a sec, Hannah." Covering the mouthpiece, she looked up at Max, and politely said, "Dinner will be fine. My address is on your Rolodex." She tried on a smile, but the edges crumbled. Not so with Max: he sported a grin with enough voltage to light up a stadium, but it was the gleam in his eye that really made

Jane uncomfortable. "I'll see you around seven-thirty," she said in a tone of dismissal.

"Seven-thirty then, *Amber.*"

After he left, Jane practically growled into the phone.

"What's all that about?" Hannah asked.

"It's a long story."

"How about the condensed version over a bowl of clam chowder at Neptune's Table?"

"Wouldn't you rather go to The Golden Garter?" Jane quipped as she fingered Sherry's gold-leaf business card. Suddenly she wondered how Max had gotten a hold of it.

"You're joking. *The* Golden Garter?"

"Why? Don't tell me they're a chain?"

"This is going to be one interesting lunch. Meet us at Neptune's in twenty minutes."

"Who's 'us'?"

"Why, Sherry Devine and me, that's who."

As Jane sailed out the door of *The Alexandrian,* Max called after her not to forget her broom. She scowled at him, then pulling her down coat around her, hurried up Washington Street, turned right at King and practically flew the three blocks to Neptune's Table. The temperature hovered around freezing, but combined with a fierce wind off the Potomac River, she felt like an icicle by the time she staggered into the restaurant. Jane and Hannah had met here often for lunch since it was one of the few places that served really delicious natural food. The outside of Neptune's Table, which jutted onto King Street, resembled the deck of a ship, and the inside was appropriately decorated with rigging, sails, brass railings and memorabilia from the great sailing days. Since she was a few minutes early, Jane scooted to the ladies' room in an attempt to do something with her hair. The March wind had whipped it into a unique style, making her look as if she'd stuck her hand into a live socket. However, her cheeks had a ruddy glow, and her eyes sparkled with undeniable excitement.

Sherry Devine. How on earth was she connected with Hannah Ritchie? The stripper and the health nut? Well, they both supported the back-to-nature movement, Jane supposed. Still, it was like discovering the queen of England was best friends with Mick Jagger. It simply seemed a little off. Various scenarios occurred to Jane, and by the time Hannah and Sherry arrived, Jane was bursting with curiosity. Hannah must have known this, for she lost no time in making introductions.

Jane was momentarily speechless. *This* was the exotic dancer? Where were the bangles, spangles, false eyelashes and flashy clothes? She was the opposite of everything Jane had expected. Although she went by the name of Sherry Devine, she said she was really Sharon Devereaux. Soft spoken and attractive, Jane guessed her to be somewhere in her mid-thirties. Sherry's figure was nicely camouflaged by a bulky cream-colored sweater and dark green slacks. Although her silver-blond hair was pulled back in a pony tail, it undoubtedly looked gorgeous under lights. She wasn't that tall either, but then Jane was five-nine, so it was hard for her to judge. As for makeup, even Hannah wore more than Sherry did.

While they were studying the menu, Jane glanced covertly from Hannah to Sherry and back again. Hannah looked the same as always. Indeed, Hannah looked the same as she had ten years ago when Jane had met her at an astrology fair in San Francisco. The woman simply didn't age; perhaps it was all that health food she kept trying to get Jane to eat. Maybe it was being married to an acupuncturist. Whatever it was, Hannah, long and lean with a radiant olive complexion and waist-length chestnut-brown hair, appeared much younger than her thirty eight years. She had an abundance of energy and ran the most efficient health-food store Jane had ever seen.

"Okay Janey, quit staring at Sherry as if she were a ghost." Hannah rapped her menu against the table, then let out a hearty laugh. "Let's order. I've been unloading cases of broccoli all morning and I'm starved."

By the time the oysters on the half shell arrived, Jane was ravenous for both food and information. She'd had enough small talk.

"My boss gave me your business card," Jane said by way of warming up to the subject. "And I have to say I think it misrepresents you. You're so . . . so—"

"Ordinary, I hope," the blonde quietly replied. "You see, I wasn't always an exotic dancer, nor was I the type to seek out charlatans like Dr. Zodiac." Sherry's hazel eyes hardened. "If circumstances had been different, I would still be in Boston, instead of—" Her gaze fell to the table.

Jane nodded slowly. "I'd like to hear your story. In fact, if you're willing *The Alexandrian* would like to print it. I hope this doesn't all sound too abrupt." She squeezed some lemon on the oysters, carefully giving Sherry time to answer.

"You're not abrupt at all. That's why I enclosed my card with that letter to the editor. I want the truth to come out, and I'll do anything I can to see that Dr. Zodiac gets what's coming to him. But then, Mr. Hunter has probably told you that already."

"Actually, he and I are having a meeting later to discuss our... plan," Jane said evasively, then paused as steaming bowls of clam chowder were set before them. So Max hadn't met Sherry. Jane felt an immediate flutter of relief, followed by a stab of annoyance at her own vulnerability. As their waiter hurried off with empty oyster plates, she added, "As for Dr. Zodiac, he's not representative of most astrologers fortunately. Don't worry, we'll find a way to expose him." Contemplating the thick chowder before her, she added, "We'll do it! Or my name isn't... Amber Starr."

"Amber Starr?" Hannah made a clucking sound. "With all the pseudonyms you dream up, you'd think you were a romance writer instead of an astrologer. But then you've been telling me for years that a Pisces has the curiosity to tackle almost anything."

"Speaking of curiosity," Jane interjected, "how did you and Sherry meet, anyway?"

"Would you believe that for four years we were bunk mates at the White Feather Camp?"

"Thirty years ago," Sherry put in with an audible sigh.

"And we sure put them through their paces, didn't we? We were finally kicked out when they caught us on one of our midnight canoe trips across the river to visit the boys' camp." On a hoot of laughter, Hannah popped half a dinner roll in her mouth.

"Thirty years ago," Sherry repeated. "And then last night, I walked into The Happy Harvest for some chamomile tea to help me sleep, and who do I find but my old bunk mate."

"We were up half the night exchanging life stories," Hannah said, digging into her salad. "And when I heard about her run-in with Alexandria's own Dr. Zodiac, I knew you all had to meet. But I had no idea the paper wanted you to do a story on it.''

"Let's just say I'm going to be working on it.''

"I'll tell you every detail I can think of,'' Sherry put in quickly, then slowly added, "However, after next week, I'm going back to Boston. I suppose you could say I've gone from riches to rags and back again, but no matter what, I'm hanging up my garter for good. Oh, but I'll be back if Dr. Zodiac is ever indicted.''

Throughout the rest of the meal, Sharon Devereaux poured out her life story, and an hour and a half later, Jane was racing up the marble steps of *The Alexandrian,* only to find the entrance blocked by Max Hunter.

"I know this is our first day of working together, but do you usually take two-hour lunches?'' Slowly he crossed his arms, then leaned against the door jamb, waiting for a reply.

"It wasn't just a lunch hour,'' she shot back, attempting to slip past him. "I was on duty!''

"*Duty?* Was it Nurse Starr? or perhaps, Police Woman Gamble?''

"You really are incorrigible. Has anyone told you that?''

"What big words you use! It must be Astrologer Smith at work.'' Max stood aside, only to snare Jane's arm as she started past. "Is 'incorrigible' an Aries or a Taurus trait?''

"Listen, I don't know about you, but this isn't my idea of a fun conversation. It's freezing out here!''

"Brisk,'' he replied, taking a deep breath. His hand was still wrapped around her arm, and though the touch was casual, it made Jane feel ridiculously light-headed.

"You are apparently wrapped in asbestos," she said, trying to extricate herself from him. Of course he was *not* wrapped in anything remotely resembling asbestos. His charcoal-gray slacks, buttoned down striped shirt and paisley tie suggested that spring really was around the corner. Still, he was too close for comfort, and despite Jane's comment about the weather, she was beginning to feel anything but cold. Being next to Max was like being near a furnace!

"If you'd like to come into my office, I'll tell you all about my lengthy lunch hour."

"Lead the way," he said, slowly releasing her arm. "Though I'm still going to hold you to dinner."

"I hadn't forgotten," she assured him. He was right behind her, and it didn't take much imagination to feel the tickle of his breath on her neck. With an energetic stride, she practically raced down the wide hall to her office. What would it take to keep Max Hunter at arm's length? When she'd accepted the job at *The Alexandrian,* she'd thought it quaint to work in a restored Victorian house; she loved being surrounded by art, Oriental carpets, high ceilings and bay windows. That was before Max Hunter arrived.

"Have a seat," she said on a note of forced levity. "I hope you don't mind if I make this brief, but I'd like to get as much as possible down on paper before I forget it."

"Called to duty and you didn't have your trusty notepad with you? Didn't tape it?"

"I didn't realize I was getting a story—well, not at first. So you can wipe that grin right off your face." Settling in her chair, Jane reached for the notepad in question and flipping to a fresh sheet, marked down the time she'd met Sherry Devine.

"Am I going to watch you scribble out more star stuff, Ms. Smith?"

Flashing Max a stern look, Jane said, "Just making a notation. Scribbling is something children do in kindergarten." Shutting the pad, she added in a softer tone, "My so-called long lunch hour was spent interviewing Sherry Devine."

"The wild goose?" Max rocked forward with such a look of surprise that it was all Jane could do to keep a reasonably straight face.

"That was a hasty judgment on my part, though from the way you went on, you led me to believe you were on intimate terms with her. What I mean is... Oh, never mind. The point is, I was so sure you were trying to lead me off Dr. Z.'s track that I acted a little paranoid. Still, you *were* right about Sherry Devine—her story's straight out of a glitzy novel. It will be a fantastic accompaniment to our Dr. Zodiac exposé." Jane knew she was grinning like the Cheshire Cat, but she couldn't help it.

"*Our* Dr. Zodiac exposé?" Max's lips twitched.

"Oh, come on. You know this is a group effort. You're taking me out to dinner to discuss it." Turning on her computer, she slanted him a smile. "We can go to Fast Eddie's. They have great subs."

"Fast Eddie's? You have quite a sense of humor, Ms. Starr—"

"Smith. I like to be Smith on Mondays."

"I've changed my mind. *I'll* choose the restaurant."

"You don't like waitresses on roller skates? Got something against Elvis Presley?"

"I was born in the fifties. I have no reason to want to return. So you can put away your crinoline and cinch belt, and—"

Jane's door suddenly swung open and Rufus appeared. "Sorry to interrupt, but the new equipment has arrived."

"At last! Now we can join the twentieth century and really get down to printing a newspaper." Max crossed the room in two strides, paused for a split second in the doorway and blew Jane a kiss. "Until tonight, *Ms. Smith.*"

"The man is...is...impossible," she muttered to the blank computer screen. If only she *did* have a crinoline and cinch belt.... Pushing the thought aside, she began typing. With any luck, she'd finish the Devine story that afternoon, interruptions notwithstanding. Immediately, the phone rang.

"Janey?...Hannah, here. I've just got a moment before our tortilla shipment comes in. But I wanted to run this idea by you."

"Shoot."

"I'm going to hire that Zodiac creep myself, request one of his women astrologers—and by God, it better be you—then together we can get all the proof you need." Hannah gave one of her characteristic hoots of laughter. "What do you think?"

"I think you're brilliant! Only wish I'd thought of it. What's Nicky going to say?"

"Oh, you know Nicky. He's behind me one hundred percent. Just imagine what an ill-placed acupuncture needle would do to Dr. Zodiac."

"That bad?"

"Nicky could send him around the moon! Gotta run. Tortillas are calling. But you get on the horn with Astroscope and make them hire you."

Jane waited for the disconnect sound, then punched in Dr. Zodiac's number. This time she not only got

straight through to him, but set up an appointment for
the following afternoon. Oh yes, he remembered her
well. Jane however, didn't like his intonation or the fact
that he referred to her as his reincarnated Amazon
queen. She had nothing against Amazons or queens, but
being tied to Dr. Z. in a past life was not a palatable
thought. Quickly, she phoned Hannah's answering machine and left a go-ahead message.

Max, Rufus and two of the guys that ran the main
press spent the afternoon laboring over the recently arrived components that would take them out of the Ice
Age of printing. By the time they'd finished, Max barely
had time for a shower and shave before picking up Jane.
Yet his mood verged on jubilant. Not only was he having dinner with "Ms. Smith," but he'd gotten hold of
Astroscope's storehouse address and if all went as
planned, he'd find out a bit more about Dr. Zodiac that
very evening. He was whistling "Singin' in the Rain"
and clearing off his desk when Rufus entered.

"Well, you're certainly chipper. Manual labor must
agree with you," Rufus remarked, swinging his brief-
case onto Max's desk. "Myself, I prefer reporting to
monkeying around on the mechanical end."

"Your help was appreciated," Max said as he con-
templated a stack of papers. Abruptly he shoved them
into a drawer, then after a beat said, "Have you ever
seen Jane's office...? Of course, you have. Amazing
woman. All those little piles of paper, and the
books—"

"I read somewhere that creative people are often surrounded by chaos. I find that oddly comforting." With
a chuckle, Rufus withdrew a single sheet of paper and
slipped it onto Max's desk. "The preliminary study you

wanted on area astrologers. Some seem legit, some flaky. Most have their own angle that they claim is infallible. But a few, including our own Ms. Gamble, are level-headed. Didn't get any real reaction to Dr. Zodiac.''

''I take it astrologers don't have a qualifying exam they have to pass.'' It was Max's turn to chuckle. ''Buyer beware, right?''

''Something like that. I'll leave the report, and we can discuss Astroscope in the morning. I'll also be curious to hear about Jane's lunch with Sherry Devine.'' He started for the door then added, ''You're not still against her working for Dr. Z., are you?''

''Would it do any good if I were?'' With a laugh, Max added, ''She's been trying to get a hold of that man all afternoon, so I think it a moot point what my feelings are. However, I have to agree with you.'' He paused to glance at Rufus's report. ''But before I let Ms. Gamble in on the good news, I'm going to do a little investigating of my own…tonight.'' Tossing the paper back onto the desk, he added, ''I guess the bottom line is, I don't like the idea of her being in any kind of danger.''

''You're kidding!'' Rufus adjusted his glasses. ''Jane Smith practically has a black belt in karate, and she never goes anywhere without her two dogs, one of which is a mammoth German shepherd named Pluto. So I wouldn't worry about her too much, if I were you. Besides, it's not as if you're sending her into a den of murderers.''

''No, just into Dr. Zodiac's lair!''

''Hire a body guard for her,'' Rufus said, heading once more for the door.

''Not a bad idea,'' Max called after him. ''How about you for the job?''

"Me?" Rufus nearly tripped. "You want *me* to guard Jane?"

"Yes. Jane and her two dogs. Hell, you don't have to actually guard her. Just sort of follow her."

"Like out of a film noire, right?"

"Right. You can even wear a trench coat if you want."

"You know, for someone who was about to wring her neck this morning, not to mention fire her, you've done an interesting about-face. Maybe *you* should be doing the following."

"I'll be keeping tabs on her," Max assured him. "But I've also got a newspaper to run. You'll be working side by side with her anyway, so it won't seem too out of the ordinary."

"Okay, okay. I'll do it." Rufus paused at the door. "You might as well tell me right now where you're taking her to dinner. Just think of it as a time saver for your old pal."

"The Water View Inn," Max replied, somewhat testily.

"Oh?"

"For dinner!"

"Right, Chief." With a mock salute, Rufus slipped out the office.

"You're late," Jane cheerfully informed Max as she opened the door. For a moment he just stared at her. Dressed in russet-colored silk, she seemed to flicker like a flame.

"I know." His reply was abrupt, but the thought of explaining how his car had broken down was more than he could bear. The grease on his hands was damning testimony anyway.

"Car trouble?" The lilt in her voice was well matched by the impish light in her eyes. "We can take Blue Gem, if you like."

"Blue Gem?"

"Oh, it's not as fast as my broom mind you, but a little more comfortable. It's my ten-year-old car. You know, the one I keep stocked with Japanese champagne." Stepping back into the foyer, she said, "C'mon in. I've got some heavy-duty hand soap somewhere."

As he followed her down the hall, a low growl, punctuated by a shrill yap, brought Max to a full stop.

"Pluto! Toto! Behave!" Crouching, she held out her arms as the largest German shepherd Max had ever seen galloped into view.

"You sure you didn't name him Cujo?" Max asked after a beat.

"Very funny." Jane held fast to the shepherd's collar. "Heel, Pluto!" Instantly the dog obeyed. "You too, Toto!"

"Pluto? Toto?" Max repeated with mild amusement. Immediately both dogs began to bark, and to Max's surprise, Toto appeared out of nowhere and tried to climb him. In vain Jane repeated her commands, but both dogs, delighted with the stranger playfully tackled him. They then streaked into the living room, leaving a trail of scattered Oriental rugs and one overturned table in their wake.

"Oh, now see what you've done!" Jane muttered as she pursued them.

"What *I've* done?" Max queried, following closely behind her. "Looks like those dogs take after their mistress." Although he chuckled as Jane chastised the dogs, he had to admit she managed them well.

He was also surprised at how neat her town house was. The parlor's furnishings, which were simple yet elegant, matched the Federal architecture. Two small velvet loveseats sat at right angles to a fireplace. A dark oak clock ticked quietly on the mantle, above which hung a portrait of an austere old woman in black velvet. Built-in bookshelves surrounded her, which seemed oddly fitting. Then of course, there was the pile of Oriental rugs and the overturned table, but not a single unfiled paper in sight.

"They'll be all right now," Jane said as she straightened from her crouched position on the floor. Then, keeping a firm grip on both dogs, she moved toward Max. "They're really quite good, except when they get around children and certain adults."

"I take it I'm one of the offending adults."

"Let's just say they know a pushover right away." As she flashed Max a brilliant smile, he wasn't sure whether to consider himself flattered or not. "Shake hands, Pluto, this is Max. *Friend!*"

"If you said enemy, would I be chopped liver?" Max asked with a laugh as he extended his hand in greeting.

"That's one way of putting it. Now, if you'll just hold them for a minute, I'll restore a little order." Patting the dogs on the head, she handed them over to Max. He grinned back at her, then looking at the dogs said, *"Friend."*

After straightening the living room, Jane gave the dogs a treat while Max cleaned the car grease from his hands at the kitchen sink. Without appearing too nosy, he took a quick inventory and was further impressed with the sparkle and shine of her kitchen. A round oak table and several ladderback chairs filled a small dining niche, which apparently led onto a back porch.

"Well," Jane said, tossing him a towel, "the last thing I remember eating was a bowl of clam chowder at one o'clock, so I'm ready for some dinner!"

"Hey, I'm really sorry about being late."

"Maybe you ought to get one of those Japanese cars," she said sassily as she slipped into a swirling turquoise cape.

"I have one of those Japanese cars. However, I think we'll manage."

"Manage" was putting it mildly, Jane thought as they glided up Washington Street in Max's magic carpet. The car was fire-engine red and it positively purred. What else, for an Aries?

"Your car didn't seem to suffer any irreparable damage," she remarked as they zipped onto the George Washington Parkway. "I must say I'm surprised."

"I'm full of surprises."

Settling back in the leather seat, Jane merely said, "Me, too." Was it her imagination or did Max bristle at her response? Well, he knew she'd intended on reaching Dr. Z. And since he was no idiot, surely he'd put two and two together. Though even he would be surprised at the plan Hannah and she had concocted.

By the time they arrived at the restaurant, Jane had smoothly steered the conversation in Max's direction by plying him with questions about his childhood. But what had started as a ploy, quickly gripped her imagination as he regaled her with tales of his prank-filled youth. Despite the amusing stories, Max was a real working man whose roots stretched back almost a hundred years to when his immigrant great-grandfather had founded *The Alexandrian*. That fact alone made him interesting.

"Still hungry?" He was standing above her in the gravel driveway of The Water View Inn, leaning on the car door, grinning. Jane felt her heart do a ridiculous lurch.

"I thought I said Fast Eddie's," she tossed off lightly as she got out of the car.

"You did, and I said to forget it. If you don't like the food there's always the view, or so they told me over the phone. Our reservations are in one of the Panorama rooms."

As Max took her arm, fluttery feelings seem to erupt all over her.

"The Panorama rooms? That sounds . . . scenic." She sounded like a moron! His grip tightened on her arm as they stepped onto a gang plank. Snapping to, Jane suddenly said, "This place just opened last month. Hannah and I have been meaning to come."

"I thought you might like it," he remarked as they entered the floating restaurant. "It should almost be as much fun as Fast Eddie's."

Slanting him what she knew was a wicked look, Jane couldn't resist teasing him. "And I thought that you being an Aries, would have gone for waitresses on roller skates."

"I dream about them every night."

"Typical."

"Any special reason?"

"Aries really go for speed. Anything fast and hot." With a pert smile she turned and followed the maitre d'.

"Must be why I'm with you, Amber," Max whispered in her ear. Jane's blush deepened as he added, "Think it's because you're my lucky star?"

Chapter Three

"You were right about the view," Jane acknowledged as she scooted into her chair.

"Your stars look pretty good." With a sweep of his hand, Max indicated the heavens. "And it's not bad of the river and the monuments, either."

"The Jefferson Memorial's my favorite," she commented, thankful that the conversation was turning to a neutral topic.

"Mine, too."

Jane muttered a politeness and turned away from Max's laser-blue eyes to look out the window. The reflection of the stars on the river, mingled with the sparkling white monuments, made for a stunning vista.

It was Max however, that occupied Jane's thoughts. Although she wasn't sure what tack to take, one thing was certain: he wasn't made of cold marble. Nor was he the brooding, silent type, he was an Aries she reminded herself, one used to going after what he wanted and getting it. He'd obviously done it all his life and been successful. His current challenge unfortunately, was her. Point one—he didn't want her on the Astroscope story and would probably stop at nothing short of tying her up. Point two—when he'd thought she was Greta Gamble, he'd wanted to fire her.

"Hey Lucky, let's order."

"Lucky?" She didn't like the gleam in his eye one bit. It suggested plenty of reasons for his rehiring her.

"Earth to Lucky..." The sound of Max's voice brought Jane back with a thump.

"Lucky?" she repeated.

"You know, your column 'Thank Your Lucky Stars.' Since you seem to collect pseudonyms, I thought you might want another." Max paused to glance at the menu, then off-handedly asked, "By the way, did Ms. Starr have any luck with Dr. Zodiac?"

"The special's flounder stuffed with crab," Jane said, ignoring the question. "But I think I'll have the lobster." Pulling her menu up like a shield, she rattled off a few more seafood delights before finally taking a deep breath and adding, "As for Dr. Z., maybe we can discuss him after dinner."

"Oh?" Max's eyebrows lifted at this. "Perhaps an after-dinner liqueur will make your news more palatable?"

"That's one way of looking at it," Jane replied, closing her menu. "Yes, I'll have the lobster tail and baked potato." She tried a brave smile, the one she always saved for the dentist.

"Okay. So Zodiac can be dessert. How about filling me in concerning Sherry Devine, or will the shock of that have to wait for after-dinner liqueur, too?"

"Not at all. But if I don't have some sustenance soon, I'll pass out. Then what'll you do?"

"I'll feed you, I'll feed you!" Motioning for a waiter, Max gave their order, taking care to ask for the restaurant's best Zinfandel. Passing Jane the bread basket, he said, "Okay Lucky, start talking."

It was piping-hot garlic bread and delicious. Nibbling a piece she said, "On to the synopsized version of Miss Devine's life which by the way, will appear on your desk tomorrow morning. To begin with, she's really Sharon Devereaux who up until two years ago, was married to Tommy Devereaux—"

"The millionaire race-car driver?" Max sat a little straighter, merely nodding as the waiter presented the bottle of wine.

"Thought that might interest you. Well, after he'd smashed up on the Indianapolis race track, Sherry found out he'd gambled away everything they owned. Mortgages were foreclosed on their Beacon Hill mansion and their horse farm in Kentucky."

"I remember when the story broke. But no one ever found out what became of Tommy's wife. She disappeared." Max paused to pour them both some wine.

"Thanks," Jane said, accepting her glass. "She went underground. Literally—her career began at The Art Caves, a nightclub in a quasi-exclusive section of Baltimore." Reaching for another piece of bread, she continued, "You see, Sherry had no marketable skills to speak of. She'd been born to a life of luxury and never imagined it could be any other way."

"What about her family? I mean, didn't they have money?"

"Unfortunately, this is where we bring out the violins. Her parents had been killed in a plane crash some years ago, and Sherry had foolishly turned her inheritance over to Tommy. As for other relatives, if they existed, they didn't come forth.'' Jane continued elaborating on the story, until the lobster arrived, at which point she took a breath and said, ''Maybe this story *should* wait for after-dinner liqueur!''

''Are you kidding? I want to hear how Sharon Devereaux turned to Dr. Zodiax.'' Max began dissecting the lobster tail and with a nod in Jane's direction said, ''Who, what, why, when and where, *then* you can eat.''

''Thanks a whole,'' Jane said on a quick swallow of wine. ''We can cut to the why. Simply put, Sherry, although once again successful and secure, had had it with the exotic-dance world and was looking into different avenues. Like the rest of us, she wanted to know what her future held. Astroscope promised the moon, and Dr. Z. hooked her for what he hoped was the long haul. First he did her chart, then he said that he sensed her dead husband needed to communicate with her. Next thing she knew, he was holding séances twice a week for her.''

''Where?''

''At his headquarters. Anyway, the important thing is *The Alexandrian* hasn't printed her letter yet, so he doesn't know she's on to him, nor does he know—'' Jane paused before slowly adding ''—that we know. And that we're going to do something about it.'' Squeezing some lemon onto the lobster, she enthused, ''This smells wonderful.''

''You're a very determined lady, aren't you?''

''Max, we've already been through this.'' She wagged her fork at him, then turning back to the lobster, blithely continued. ''The other amazing part of this story is that my friend Hannah went to summer camp with Sherry thirty years ago, and they've just been reunited.''

"Okay c'mon, spit it out—"

"The lobster?" Jane feigned disbelief.

"The rest of your grand plan."

"Oh, that." Poking at her baked potato as if that might buy her time, she slowly said, "Well, if you must know..."

"I must."

Carefully mashing the sour cream into the potato, she said, "I was able to get through to him....."

"And...?"

"And I have an appointment with Dr. Z. tomorrow afternoon."

"Jane—"

"Max, please don't bang on the table."

"I am not banging on the table, I'm simply—"

"But you're about to. Aries often bang things. Even in public." She shook her head. "Tsk, tsk."

"Listen, I've been looking into this Zodiac character myself, and I think he's shady."

"After what Sherry said, we know he's shady." Inspecting a forkful of potato Jane mused, "You could almost paint him black."

"That's just what I mean," Max put in hastily, then leaning over the table, he took hold of Jane's hand. "Don't you understand that until we get the lay of the land, we have no idea what kind of person we're dealing with."

Pulling her hand from his, Jane reached for her wine. Her hand still tingled where he'd held it.

"Do you hear me?"

"Loud and clear."

"You're an astrologer and a writer, not Nancy Drew or Miss Marple!" He ran his hand through his hair, then reaching for the wine bottle, poured them both a second glass.

"Let's not quibble. You want to get a clear picture of Dr. Z. before sending me into the lion's den. Well, Sherry's already gotten his number. He performs incredible parlor tricks at these séances, really plays on people's fears and superstitions. I also bet he's laughing all the way to the bank. You know, if we get a good scoop out of this, we'll have Sherry to thank."

"Promise me you won't see Zodiac without stopping by my office first thing in the morning."

"Good heavens, are you checking the man out tonight?"

"Just do as I say."

"When the Ram bleats, the sheep bows. Or something like that." She sent Max her most radiant smile.

Max was also on a mission tonight, and unless Jane was much mistaken, it would begin after he left her off. Only tonight, she resolved, he would have a shadow.

Dinner concluded with a stroll down The Water View's pier, which jutted into the Potomac River. With the soft lapping sounds of water all around them and the canopy of stars above, Jane had to admit it was a magical night. The wind had died down, though the air was still brisk.

"Chilly?" Max didn't wait for her reply, but slipped his arm around her and drew her against him.

He didn't wait for anything, but surely Jane should know that about an Aries man by now. And as much as she hated to admit it, she reveled in his Aries spirit. When she felt his grip tighten slightly on her upper arm, Jane's heart skipped a beat.

"That's the Big Dipper," Max said softly, pointing to the constellation overhead.

"I thought you didn't know anything about stars," Jane heard herself reply.

"That was astrology, my dear, not astronomy. On a clear night, anyone can find the Dippers."

"I—I suppose you're right." She was acutely aware of his touch, his nearness and of the way her bones felt as though they were dissolving. She'd long since given up on her heart; it was doing double time. The lump in her throat kept her from talking, and at this point, maybe that was a good thing since there was no telling what she might say.

This seemed to suit Max fine. He took her by the shoulders and gently turned her toward him. One finger slipped beneath her chin as his lips lowered to meet hers, only to stop and hover just inches from them. His hands cupped her chin, and his thumbs made lazy patterns against her cheeks.

"Well, Lucky," he said hoarsely, "next time out we can try Fast Eddie's, and instead of hearing Sherry Devine's life story, I'd like to hear yours. Something tells me it's pretty interesting."

"Oh, I doubt it can compare to hers." Jane tried to steady her breathing, but how could she when he seemed about to kiss her? The crazy part was, she didn't know whether she wanted it or not.

Max knew what he wanted; he'd known from the moment he'd met her. He wanted *her;* plain Jane Smith.

He stepped back a pace, then with an inward shudder, let his hands drop to his side, only to abruptly lean forward and kiss her forehead. The way her hands flew up and pressed lightly against his jacket made him feel a little high, and it had nothing to do with the wine. Jane would undoubtedly say it was because of the planets, and who knows? Maybe it was.

Once back at her town house, Jane waited until Max had gotten back into his car, then she and the dogs got into hers and were off in pursuit of him.

He'd turned onto Patrick Street, so she figured he was probably headed for the warehouse area. If Jane's ESP was off course and this didn't have something to do with Astroscope, she'd return to straight reporting. Well, whatever Max's destination, she was not far behind. One thing about his red Acura, it would be pretty easy to keep in sight.

"Just as I thought," Jane told her canine companions as they turned off Patrick Street and took the bridge over the railroad tracks. Pluto perked up his ears and let out an acknowledging bark. Being a shepherd, he enjoyed these little "tours of duty," as Jane called their frequent jaunts, and he especially liked having conversations with his mistress. Toto, while tolerating it, much preferred romping in the park.

"Ah ha!" Jane exclaimed, making an almost immediate sharp left off Route 1. "We're getting warmer. And I'm sure glad you guys are with me." The surrounding neighborhood consisted mainly of shuttered warehouses and shacks. Several streetlights were out, and the ones lit were little consolation. If her parents could see her now.... No point in thinking about that.

Her father had been one of the top newsmen in TV and knew only too well how rampant crime was in the Washington D.C. area. He'd not approved of her move to Alexandria. He felt that normal people lived in Connecticut and got jobs that made sense; casting people's horoscopes and writing a column on the blasted stuff didn't qualify. Pops could have gotten Janey a newscaster job with one of the networks: a safe, sensible job where she could report all the horrible crimes that happened to other people in other places—but never endanger herself.

"No point in thinking about that," Jane muttered as she slowed the car to keep pace with Max. "I am what I am—despite Pops. And certainly despite Max Hunter."

Pluto gurgled a growl in response.

"Well, it's true. I don't know who that Max thinks he is. Fires me one minute. Wines, dines and practically kisses me the next. But he didn't kiss me...well, not really." Jane sniffed. Heavens knows what she'd have done if he had. "No point in thinking about that, either. Hey Pluto, I think we've just arrived." Immediately dimming her lights, she pulled into a parking space some distance from Max's car. "Shh. Not a sound!" Her heart was making enough noise as it was. "We'll give him three minutes, then we're going in." In the darkened car, Jane couldn't help smiling; she really did sound like *Police Woman*.

Max paused to eye the building. This was Astroscope's main warehouse? It was nothing more than a dilapidated garage. The siding was rusted and on closer inspection, so was the padlock. Walking around to the side, he managed to jimmy open a window and after some maneuvering, he slipped inside. No burglar alarms went off. So far so good, he thought, checking his stained and ripped shirt.

The inside of Dr. Z.'s storehouse seemed as dark as the black hole of Calcutta, and unfortunately the batteries in Max's flashlight were about to give out. He'd better make good use of his time he decided, moving forward.

As for the stench of mildew, he could live with that. He didn't know what he hoped to find, but if it was there he'd find it. Five years as a senior investigative reporter had taught him a few things. His light, scanning across the room revealed shrouded shapes and a small catwalk flush with the wall. As Max swung his light to inspect it, something or someone moved quickly toward the ladder. Max countering with a move of his own, tripped over a coil of rope. As he stumbled to recover his balance, he felt the crack on the back of his head, and all was darkness.

"Okay Pluto, let's go!" Jane said, snapping the lead onto his collar. "Max has had enough time." At Pluto's bark, she added, "I know he won't like it, but that's too bad. Toto, you stand guard here."

As they neared the garage, Pluto began to lunge forward, which probably meant trouble. Seeing the padlocked entrance, they hurried around to the side. The window, several feet from the ground was gaping open. The shepherd strained at the lead, and Jane quickly set him free.

"Go on, boy!" He knew immediately what she meant and in a fluid leap, bounded through the open window. Jane, setting a nearby trash can beneath it, hoisted herself up and quickly scrambled through. The inside was pitch black, and except for Pluto's barking, as silent as a tomb. As she landed with a thud and staggered forward, the dog came to her aid. But where was Max? Tentatively she called his name. Nothing. Prickly panic shot up her spine as she inched forward. Darn, why hadn't she thought to bring a flashlight? Even Nancy Drew had one.

Suddenly Pluto let out a howl, then gently taking Jane's hand in his mouth, pulled her forward until she stumbled into something. The dog howled again, then plopped down on all fours and began to whine.

Jane sank down beside him and groping, found a flashlight. She snatched it up and aiming it directly in front of her, let out an involuntary cry as its beam fell on Max's face. He was unconscious, his color ashen, but, thank God, he was breathing. She had no idea what to do, but instinctively she began to chafe his wrists and call his name—that always worked in the books she'd read. But when nothing happened, she gave him several taps on the cheek. Almost immediately his eyes blinked open, then with a groan they closed again.

"Max! Max, it's Jane." She pulled the flashlight back a bit, and gently ran her fingers across his brow. "Can you hear me?"

"Yes," he mumbled somewhat thickly as he tried to pull himself to a sitting position, but Jane held him back.

"No! Just rest for a moment."

"Why?"

"Because I want to make sure you don't have any broken bones." Pluto kept whimpering as he nuzzled Max's arm.

"Broken bones? What the devil are you..." He paused as if a vague memory were struggling to surface. "Did the lights go out again?" he muttered after a moment.

"Again?" What on earth was he talking about? Oh, God, maybe he was in shock. "Well, lights do have a way of going off and on."

"Damn house is too old.... Wiring came in with Edison."

"Ancient," Jane agreed. Oh Lord, his eyes were closed again. There was no telling how bad off he was. No doubt about it, she'd have to get him out of there. Nicky would know what to do.

"Max...Max?" At his nodded assent, she was somewhat encouraged. "We need to get out of here."

"Need new presses, is what we need."

"That too. But, well, you see you've...you've had a fall—"

"I have?" His eyes snapped open and as he tried moving he added, "So I have. But who are— Oh, I remember, Jane...Jane...Gambler."

"That's right," she replied carefully.

"Had a fall...? Where the dickens are we, anyway?"

"In a garage. Don't ask questions now. Just lie still while I try to find the exit. Pluto will be with you. You know, he's the one who really found you."

"Who the hell is Pluto?"

"You remember my dog, don't you?" No, he obviously didn't remember him. "That's Pluto," she added, shining the light on the dog. "I'll be right back after I find an exit." She hadn't gone ten feet before a chilling thought struck her: what if someone had knocked Max out and was still lurking about? The possibility propelled her toward the back of the garage and an exit. Thank heavens it was locked from the inside. After a few minutes, Jane had slid back the dead bolt and thrown open the double doors.

Max was remarkably agreeable, too agreeable and certainly not his usual Aries self. She knew he felt awful—one look at the bump on his head told her that—so after making sure he didn't have any broken bones, she managed to haul him to his feet and get him outside and into her car. Leaving Pluto with him, she returned to the garage for a quick check. If there had been anyone, he'd fled, but since she needed to rebolt the entrance anyway, she figured she might as well have another look.

Her curiosity paid off in spades. A few feet from where Max had been knocked out, Jane discovered a large sandbag. Aiming the flashlight's beam upward, she saw several similar sandbags haphazardly tied to a catwalk. Something or someone had loosened the rope, sending one down on top of Max. She'd check out this place later, but for now Max needed attention. Afterwards, she'd cycle back and pick up his car.

By the time they turned onto Nick and Hannah's street, Max seemed a bit more coherent, although he was still hazy about where they'd been. From the little Jane could gather, his memory stopped short of their dinner date. So much for the dazzling impression she'd thought she'd made.

"Where are we?" he asked as Jane pulled in back of Hannah's van.

"We're here!" she replied cheerfully as she clicked off the ignition.

"Where's *here?*" Max tried to turn his head, but a sharp pain made him think twice about it.

"Nick and Hannah Ritchie's. You'll be fit as a fiddle when they get through with you."

Managing a sideways glance at Jane, Max wondered if her presence doomed him to terminal confusion.

"Fit as a fiddle," she repeated, giving his hand a pat. Then stuffing her car keys into her purse, she positively beamed at him.

He was also confused by the presence of the dogs. The little one at his feet seemed intent on chewing his shoes, while the cold nose of the Goliath in the back seat seemed permanently attached to Max's ear. Where did these animals come from? They weren't at the party, were they?

"C'mon Pluto, Toto!" Jane called as she bounded from the car.

Pluto. Of course, he must be the German shepherd Rufus had told him about. But *Toto?* Well, they weren't in Kansas, that was for sure.

"Now, just lean on me like you did before," she said, swinging his door open. Before Max knew what was happening, Jane had hooked her arm around him and was muttering encouraging words to him. Hell's bells! Maxwell Hunter was being hauled around by a woman and two dogs!

"Much better!" she enthused. The dogs barked. Max groaned. Somehow they managed to get to the front door. Maybe he had died, he thought morosely. The problem was, he didn't know if this was heaven or hell. His head felt like hell, but the woman felt like heaven. *Jane Gambler...?* No, that wasn't right. *Jane Starr?* They had reached the front door of wherever they were going, and he still wasn't sure of her name—or of anything else, for that matter. *Greta,* that was it. *Greta Gamble.* A sudden flood of memories caught him off guard. He'd fired her, rehired her, argued with her, been driven crazy by her and... kissed her?

Just as the front door opened, a hissing white Persian leapt from the arms of the woman who greeted them. There was a lot of barking and hissing, and then that damn black wave came up again, and Max supposed he must have momentarily lost consciousness.

"Max! Max!" Someone was calling his name.

"Let's get him over here," a male voice said.

He felt himself being lifted onto a bed, then someone was loosening his tie, taking off his belt, shoes and socks. Struggling to sit up he managed to say, not without some humor, "I'm still here. Must have blacked out back there."

"Don't worry Max, everything is going to be all right. I've filled Nick in, so he'll know where to put the needles." Jane smiled down at him, then turning to the couple next to her said, "And this is Nick and Hannah."

"Nick and Hannah," Max mumbled, still attempting to sit up. "Where are we?"

"At their house," Jane informed him as she put a restraining arm across his chest. "You had a bad blow to your head Max, so you need to rest."

"Oh... Now I'm beginning to remember...." He sank back and ran a shaky hand through his hair. He was beginning to remember that he couldn't recall one damn thing about a blow to the head, although other pieces of the puzzle were beginning to fit together. Of course, there was no real order to it, and the effort to make sense of the evening only seemed to aggravate his headache.

"What the devil am I doing in someone else's house?" he asked after a beat.

The woman who'd answered the door patted his hand, and said softly, "You're recuperating. Now, if you'll just turn your head, I'm going to clean some of the blood away and put a bandage on that cut."

No one had bandaged Max since he fell down in the fourth grade and broke his nose. No one had patted his hand since then either, and now in the space of an evening *two* women had! But then he'd never been knocked unconscious.

Rolling his head to the side, he was greeted by the ever-alert Pluto. The dog's almond-shaped eyes had an almost human quality about them, and they were boring straight into Max. *"Friend,"* Max murmured, then he winced as Hannah swabbed his head and wondered if he had amnesia. "Five-Seven-Five-Nine-Zero-Five-Three—"

"Sorry if I'm hurting you," Hannah said. "It'll just be a few minutes longer."

"No problem. I was just seeing if I could remember my Social Security number. Of course, I won't know if it's right till I check."

"Now, if you'll just lift your head a little, I'm going to tie the gauze around in front."

"Sure thing," Max replied, trying to ignore the pounding in his skull.

"There!" Hannah said, after she put the finishing touches to his bandage. "You're all ready for Nicky." Then turning to Jane she added, "That's some head gear, don't you think?"

"He looks like Lawrence of Arabia after a bad night," Jane answered on a laugh, and moved closer to Max. "Do you want a mirror?"

"I think it can wait till I get home," Max muttered.

"Oh, you're not going home yet," Jane informed him. "Nick is upstairs getting his needles ready."

"He is, is he?" Max took in a deep breath. "Getting ready to work his *magic* on me? Sort of like voodoo, I suppose."

"Don't be silly! Nicky's an acupuncturist. The best in the area."

"*An acupuncturist.* Oh, *those* kind of needles."

"I'll fix a cup of camomile tea for you," Hannah offered, quickly crossing to the kitchen.

"You know," Jane said in hushed tones, "you don't have to look as if you're about to be tortured! Acupuncture is a respected tool of healing. And besides, Nick is also a naturopath."

"Is that like being a Virgo?"

"No! But if I didn't know better, I'd say you were the Virgo."

"And what's *that* supposed to mean?"

"You're being very prickly, Mr. Hunter."

On a sudden laugh Max said, "Ah, but Ms. Gamble, wouldn't the prospect of being stuck full of needles bring out *your* prickly side?"

Chapter Four

"That isn't so bad, now is it?" Jane purred twenty minutes later from her perched position near Max's head.

"Except that I feel like a porcupine," he grumbled back. Then to Nicky, who was taking his pulse, he added, "But whatever you're doing, thanks, because I have to admit I do feel better. The headache has subsided somewhat, but I still can't remember this evening."

"All in good time. You know, that was quite a blow you took." Nicky's dark eyes crinkled in a warm smile, then moving quickly to the other side of Max he said, "But you're responding well, and with a little patience you'll be back on your feet in no time."

"Patience isn't one of my long suits," Max confessed. I'm also running out of sanity, he thought staring at a sky-blue ceiling decorated with angels. This definitely was not Potomac Hospital. If his memory of the living room served him right, perhaps they'd been caught in a time warp. He remembered seeing turn-of-the-century mannequins in wedding attire stationed by the front door, a scaled-down merry-go-round where there should have been a coffee table, a pile of brightly colored pillows where there should have been a couch, and matching Indian bedspreads draped across the broad windows. Looking up from the massage mat, he now saw an anatomy chart juxtaposed with a framed poster of George Harrison that hung above the fireplace. The mantel held candles, crystals *and* a smiling, living, breathing yellow cat. Max knew it was alive because it switched its tail and licked its chops.

"Wasn't it the Chinese who perfected slow torture?" Max idly asked as another needle hit the spot. He'd be damned if he'd so much as say ouch.

"Sorry about that," Nick said. "We're just dispersing a little energy. Not to worry. This should help you regain your memory."

Max managed a tight smile as he thought of the kind of headline his old paper, the *Dallas Post* favored: Editor of *The Alexandrian* becomes human pin cushion after total lapse of memory.

"Max is an Aries," Jane announced as Nick palpated Max's wrist for a pulse.

"It's still there, isn't it?" Max asked, his curiosity getting the better of him.

"Definitely. In fact, considering what you've been through, I'm surprised the triple heater is doing so well."

"Triple heater? It's all Greek to me."

"No, more like Chinese," Jane put in, leaning closer to him. Out of the corner of his eye, Max saw the shimmer of her red curls, and on a deep breath, he took in the faint floral scent she was wearing. Moving his head for a better look was out of the question since needles protruded from both sides of his neck.

"That doesn't explain triple heater," Max said after a while.

"Another time," Nick replied. "It's a little complicated."

"Which probably means it's tied up with ancient Chinese philosophy, right?"

"Right you are," Nick answered cheerfully as he swabbed Max's ankle with alcohol. "Now to be on the safe side, I'm going to put in two more needles."

"Oh, for the triple heater?"

"No. Kidney/gall bladder. Now this might be a little sensitive," Nick warned as he inserted the first needle.

"No problem," Max said through gritted teeth. "No problem at all," he repeated as the second needle went in. "But why do you keep taking my pulse?"

"Come to one of my classes," Nick answered with a chuckle as he checked the pulses once again.

"Nicky's Intensive Oriental Healing is fascinating," Jane broke in. "I took it when I first came here. You see," she continued, inching closer to Max, "there are six pulses on each wrist, which correspond to the twelve meridians in your body—"

"Which are undoubtedly related to the twelve signs of the zodiac," Max said flippantly.

"Well, as a matter of fact," Nick said as he made a notation in his chart, "they do relate to Oriental astrology. But that's something we'll have to discuss another time." Shutting the chart he reached for Max's wrist again, then after a moment said, "Excellent!"

Max wanted to say that despite what the triple heater was or wasn't doing, he still didn't remember what had happened to him. As for lying on a massage mat and being punctured with little needles while three humans, two dogs, several cats and a parrot watched . . . he concluded that perhaps he'd lost *more* than his memory.

He'd always thought of himself as sensible. Good Lord, he suddenly felt as though he'd been drinking too much champagne again. He could barely keep his eyes open. Nick said something to him about going to Chicago, then left the room. The next time Max looked up, he was alone except for the little terrier, who had snuggled up against his side, and the ever reliable Pluto, who was once again breathing down his neck.

"Mission accomplished!" Jane said on a jubilant note as she tossed Max's car keys onto the kitchen table. Then peeking around the corner into the living room, she asked in hushed tones, "Do you think he's still asleep?"

"He's been out like a light the whole time you were gone." Hannah cocked her head to one side and observed her friend quietly for a moment before adding, "You didn't tell me that Robert Redford was your new boss—"

"Hey, I haven't had time to catch my breath, let alone fill you in with romantic details."

"Ah-ha! So you do admit to something more than just—" She waved her hand in the air then whispered, "All work and no play!"

"Right. I just love trailing men to darkened storehouses and playing Mrs. Kojac!" Tiptoeing into the living room, Jane went to where Max was sleeping peacefully.

"Your friend however, did mumble in his sleep," Hannah said softly. "Something about Nancy Drew . . ."

"He's obsessed." Jane gave Toto who was gazing inquiringly at her, a pat on his head. "Well, at least he's well protected," she mused, noting the army of curious felines sprawled about the room. "Max is going to be...okay, isn't he?"

"Oh, you of little faith!"

"No, just a Pisces prone to fretting."

"And I'll bet you asked Nicky the same question, didn't you?"

With a laugh, Jane nodded. "He said Max had the constitution of an ox and we'd probably have to tie him down tomorrow! I suppose that figures, for as innocent as he looks right now, he's really hell on wheels."

"That bad? C'mon out to the kitchen, girl," Hannah said, grabbing her friend's hand. "He'll probably be waking up in fifteen minutes or so, but in the meantime, take a load off your feet, cause we've got some catching up to do on the Astroscope case while I prep some veggies."

"What's this, grocer turned private eye?" With a laugh, Jane followed her friend into the kitchen. She pulled a stool up to the counter and watched as Hannah unloaded a sack of carrots from the refrigerator.

"Well, between all those mysteries you lend me and our own real-life drama, can you blame me? After all, it's a little more exciting than working a cash register." Brandishing a carrot at her friend, Hannah added, "Okay Janey, your news first then mine. Come on...what's up?"

"Everything!" Propping her elbows on the counter top and leaning forward, Jane felt a wave of excitement crest inside her. "To begin with, your doll of a husband insisted on going into the storehouse with me, and he agrees—"

"Jane Smith! You said you were just going to pick up Max's car—"

"Oh come on, Hannah. I couldn't pass up another peek at Astroscope's storehouse! And now I think I know a little more about how Dr. Z. operates."

"Okay, Okay! I'm all ears," Hannah said, putting her knife to one side.

"Well, if I'm not mistaken, he's running a real high-tech operation. And I think I've got the photos to prove it." Absently Jane reached for a chunk of carrot and began nibbling it.

"What did you find?"

"On first glance, it looked like Dr. Zodiac was into little theater—you know, masks, wigs, stage makeup and costumes from just about every imaginable period in history. Then there were the stage lights, sound equipment, microphones *and*—" Feeling a sudden rush of adrenaline, Jane took a deep breath. "Get this. I think he uses holograms to produce his ghosts!"

"Not to be ignorant, but what exactly is a hologram?"

"Now, you know I'm not the most technical person in the world, but from this mystery I read last week—"

"That was fiction, Janey, this is real life," Hannah informed her as she retrieved her knife and continued chopping carrots.

"Hey, I know the difference."

"So what's a hologram?"

"Well, in a mystery I've just finished, the villain tries to drive the heroine crazy with a series of staged hauntings, which are actually three-dimensional films projected into clear air. The author didn't go into technical details, but it certainly sounded feasible." Absently, Jane took another bite of carrot.

"I suppose that would explain how Dr. Z. managed to resurrect Tommy Devereaux's ghost."

"Exactly. There was undoubtedly lots of film footage of Tommy—especially when he won the Indianapolis 500. So all Astroscope had to do was get a hold of some film, make a hologram of it and voila, they were able to conjure him up on command."

"Maybe you're in the wrong field after all," Hannah said as she quickly finished chopping the carrots. Then scooping them into a pot she added, "Hope your Max likes cream of carrot soup, because something tells me that tomorrow he's going to need some sustenance after he hears your theory. Mind you, I'm not knocking it." Opening the refrigerator, she slipped the pot inside. "You know, if you're hungry—"

"Heavens, I don't even want this." Jane regarded the carrot stub with a jaundiced eye. "Whenever I get nervous about something, I start munching—deplorable habit." With a flick of the wrist, she popped the remainder into her mouth.

"You're nervous?"

"Anxious is what I meant. Having just stumbled onto Astroscope's props, I feel antsy to put this info to use. I suppose I'm also a bit overwhelmed."

"That's putting it mildly," Hannah agreed. "But you know something, I think you and I'd make a pretty good detective team."

"Let's be sure to tell Max first thing!" Jane exclaimed with a laugh. "Before we do that though, tell me what you thought of Dr. Zodiac."

"You and Sherry were right on target," Hannah replied as she began sponging off the kitchen counter. "And with that ridiculous goatee and mustache, he really does look like a reincarnated Spanish inquisitor. Anyway, he spent about twenty minutes with me, and I want you to know I primed the pump—told him how he was my last hope, being how I keep dreaming about my deceased husband, that I just know he's trying to tell me something about the running of our estate in Potomac, etcetera, etcetera.''

"You with an estate in *Potomac?*"

"So I'm one of those eccentric millionaires. You know, they don't all look like royalty. Let me tell you, my performance was Oscar material, right down to the tears.''

"Tears?"

"It was the only way I could get an immediate appointment. I even went so far as to tell him that I'd had a dream about what my astrologer looked like.''

"You didn't!"

"I did. Oh, don't worry. I simply said that in my dream she was a tall woman with red hair.''

"Super."

"Now, you don't have to be sarcastic. He'll never figure it out. The man's too wrapped up in himself.'' Crossing to the stove, Hannah put the kettle on. "Want some tea—the soothing variety?''

"*Something.* As it is, I'll probably be tossing and turning all night, trying to figure out our next move.''

"Our next move is all yours, remember?"

"Right! I see our man Z. tomorrow afternoon.'' Craning her neck to look around the corner and into the living room Jane added, "I wonder if Max will remember I have an appointment.''

"Time will tell," Hannah replied, tapping her foot while she waited for the water to boil.

"Better make him a cup, too. I think he's starting to wake up," Jane said, slipping off the stool. "I'm going to check on him.''

"He'll be fine," Hannah said as Jane tiptoed into the living room.

Pluto, who had positioned himself at Max's head, perked his ears up at Jane's entry, as if awaiting another command. Toto merely wagged his tail and gave his mistress a questioning look. Thankfully, Capt'n Hook, the bawdy African parrot, whose cage hung in one corner, had finally tucked in his beak for the evening.

"Well Pluto, looks like Max is still asleep, after all," Jane whispered as she sat cross-legged on the floor next to the massage mat.

"Max is *not* asleep."

"You've been faking!" Jane teased. Pluto echoed this with a throaty growl, and Toto immediately burrowed his nose under Max's outstretched hand.

"Me? Faking it? Good heavens, woman, what an accusation." Suppressing a yawn, Max stretched his arms over his head. "Though, I have felt better. What time is it, anyway?"

"A little after midnight."

"That late?"

"Do you remember what happened tonight?" Jane asked casually, checking his features for any sign of recognition.

"Am I going to be shot at dawn if I don't?"

"You *don't* remember."

"If you mean how I got knocked out—zip. Though I can still remember my Social Security number, and I know that I've just been alternatively treated, that your name is Jane Smith, that we argued about Dr. Zodiac, and that Rufus— Oh, I'd better give him a call."

"Stay put! I'll call and tell him you won't be in tonight."

"I can't stay here." Max made an attempt to sit up, only to sink back. "Damn, can you imagine Clint Eastwood taking an acupuncture break in *Dirty Harry?*"

"That was a movie. This is real life."

"You could have fooled me." As their eyes met, Max let out a sigh. "Okay, you win."

Jane was on her feet and halfway to the phone before she spun around and added, "You've been called away on assignment, right?"

"Wrong. Knowing you, I'd end up in Timbuktu."

"You must be on the mend. You're getting testy." Lifting the receiver, she smiled at him. "I'll just tell Rufus that you were knocked unconscious, my dogs and I found you, but you've lost part of your memory." Having rattled this off, she quickly dialed the number.

"You know, being around you might make a man forget all kinds of things!" Max said, even more confused.

If he stuck with her, he'd never lack for companionship, Max mused as the little terrier began a thorough washing of his hand. Life wouldn't be dull, either. And aside from her offbeat personality, she had the kind of looks that grew on him. At the moment however, she looked a little worse for wear. Her fiery curls were tangled, there were smudges on her face, and what had undoubtedly been an attractive russet silk dress was torn and stained in several places. Oblivious to her disheveled appearance, she was having quite an animated chat with Rufus. Damn! Max bet she was telling him exactly how he'd been knocked out.

"Hey!" he called out, rising up on one elbow. "I'd like to speak to him." He watched as she hurriedly spoke into the phone, then with a somewhat guilty look, hung up and slowly crossed toward him.

Before he had a chance to grumble, Hannah entered from the kitchen, carrying a tray. "Sorry to take so long. I had to hunt high and low for the tea, but it's guaranteed to put you out like a light," she said as she set the tray on a low table.

"Just what I need," Max said on a laugh as he slowly sat up.

"Nicky's certain you'll be feeling much better tomorrow," Hannah said as she placed several pillows in back of Max. "Oh, in case you're wondering, he's gone to Chicago for an acupuncture convention, but I have the telephone number, so we can always call him in case—"

"My triple heater gets too hot?" Max suggested, accepting a cup of tea.

"No problem there," Hannah assured him as she poured tea for Jane and herself.

"Well, I plan on being up tomorrow—*after* my twelve-hour observation period is over." Then with a nod in Jane's direction, he said. "I take it you gave Rufus all the details?"

"You're wondering if he knows what you don't, right?" She gave him her most devilish smile, and for a split second he had a flash of memory—they were beneath a starry sky in the middle of a river, and by God if he wasn't about to kiss her. He tried to hold the image, but it misted over, leaving only a few stars in its wake.

"I'm not wondering anything," he said, annoyed at his continued lapse of memory.

"You'll be glad to know that I got your car this evening—"

"I didn't know it was missing." Max wrinkled his nose, then took a swallow of tea. Maybe he'd be better off if he were unconscious.

"Oh, it wasn't missing. It was...it was..."

With a shrug, Jane looked to Hannah, who quickly added, "We just thought you'd like to have your car, so Nicky dropped Jane by to get it. More tea?"

"No, this is fine." Leveling his gaze at Jane, Max asked, "Shall we play Twenty Questions? I don't think I have enough energy for Charades."

"Tomorrow," Jane said, quickly swallowing the last of her tea. "Besides, it's getting late."

"Not that late," Max said, reaching for Jane's hand. It was cool to the touch and the skin was as smooth as silk.

Abruptly, she withdrew it and he felt a small pang.

"It's after twelve," she stated. "And we all could do with a good night's sleep. Aside from your bruised head, we've got a zoo that comes to life at daybreak. Finish up your tea so we can haul you off to bed."

"Whoa, woman! Wherever I'm going, it'll be under my own steam. Just point me in the right direction."

"It's across the hall. It's small but comfy, and it's got it's own bathroom. Here, let me help you up."

Waving her assistance aside, Max managed to get to his feet, only to stumble backward into the wall. Jane was at his side almost immediately, and despite his grumblings to the contrary, it made him feel pretty damn good. With a grin, he mumbled, "Clint Eastwood, huh?"

"Right. 'Go ahead. Make my day!'"

"I think you already have," he said, feeling a wave of dizziness come over him. "It's not your fault I can't remember it."

"I'll tell you everything tomorrow," Jane promised as she hooked her arm through his.

"I'll hold you to it. First thing in the morning…" Max paused as a distant bell rang in his head. *First thing in the morning* . . .

"Let's make it after lunch."

"Make it whenever you like," Hannah said, following them into the hallway. "But let's get Max horizontal."

"You know, I think my memory is starting to come back—"

"It'll come back a lot faster if you get a reasonable night's sleep," Jane urged as she gently tugged on his arm.

"Something to do with that Zodiac character," he mumbled.

"Tomorrow afternoon," he heard her say as he floated toward yet another mat on the floor. Only this one was considerably softer than the massage mat.

"You have something against beds in this house?" he asked as a fluffy down comforter was placed across him.

"They're called futons," Hannah informed him.

"Oh, right. Japanese." He struggled with his eyelids in a futile attempt to keep them open, but he felt as if cement had been poured over them.

"You've won over my dogs," Jane said softly. Then, "Good night."

He opened his mouth to reply, but she had shut out the light and gone. Idly, Max wondered if there were clouds painted on this ceiling, too.

As he drifted off to sleep, he felt two warm and furry bodies press close to him. Maybe it was all a dream; maybe he'd wake up and find himself back at the *Dallas Post*. But somehow he didn't think so, not even in his wildest dreams.

The following morning, Jane donned one of Hannah's gayly patterned Japanese kimonos, and having found Max sleeping, decided to whip up some pancakes for him. Intuitively, she didn't think he'd go for cream of carrot soup first thing. Hannah had been called to the store early to handle a crisis and had left Jane to take care of the zoo. Capt'n Hook, as usual, tried to nibble her fingers when she filled his dish, the cats serenaded her as she doled out their food and of course, Pluto and Toto put in their vocal contribution. Only the guppies remained silent.

"Shall I have to sing for my supper, also?"

Jane gave a start as she looked up from the sizzling pancakes. "Hey, what are you doing up? Last time I checked you were asleep."

"That was before the zoological chorus," Max replied with a crooked smile. "But I've showered. No razor, though..."

As he ran a hand across the blond stubble on his chin, Jane had a ridiculous desire to feel it herself.

"You probably should be back in bed," she managed to say, waving the spatula in his direction. He was wearing the man's kimono that Hannah had put out for him. It was dark blue, loosely sashed, and came to his knees. Jane could have spent the morning just looking at the man. "You know, I'd planned on bringing this in to you."

"Ah, breakfast...in futon—and served by lovely lady." He started to bow, only to pause and add, "Still a little dizzy topside."

"Your twelve hours aren't up yet," she informed him in what she hoped was a crisp, authoritative voice.

"You make me sound like a condemned man." Moving toward her, he took away the spatula, and then in a soft gravelly voice added, "How about something with caffeine in it, or is that a no-no?"

"Do you know how to cook?" Jane shot back with a toss of her head.

"You're not answering my question," he said pleasantly as he eased the spatula under the pancakes.

"Oh, you'll make a mess of them that way," she protested, grabbing at the utensil.

"Coffee, woman!" he said, moving away from her.

"You'll have to settle for Cosmic Thunder tea," she answered peevishly. "And believe me, it's got enough caffeine to wake the dead." Reaching up for the box, she plunked it down on the counter. "You're quite an Aries, you know that? Double Aries, in fact." Opening the box, she made a face at him. "'Coffee, Woman!' My name is Jane."

"Greta, Amber, Jane. See? My memory's not so bad, after all." Twirling the spatula, he moved slowly toward the stove. "I think they're ready to be turned."

"Oh, you do, do you?" With quick movements, she put the kettle on, snatched the spatula from Max, handed him the box of tea and said, "When the whistle blows, pour the water over the tea bags. I'll handle this end of breakfast."

Her smile met his and she felt her tummy do a curious flip-flop that had nothing whatsoever to do with hunger.

They kept smiling at each other, and although Jane was beginning to feel self-conscious, she would feel equally uncomfortable looking away. Then the kettle whistled and Max was free to pour the water.

Twenty minutes later, as Max scraped his plate clean of all vestiges of pancake, he let out a groan. "I thought you said this tea was going to resurrect me. Woman, that had to be the most pallid coffee substitute I've ever had."

"It wasn't a coffee substitute, and my name is Jane." With a pert nod, she jumped down from her stool and removing his plate, headed for the sink.

"I know your name, m'dear."

"Then try using it," she tossed back, sinking the sticky plates into lukewarm dishwater.

"Want me to help you dry, Greta-Jane." His voice, suddenly Southern, stretched out like molasses on a hot day.

"You're supposed to rest, remember?" Suppressing a grin, Jane began scrubbing a plate.

"I don't think drying dishes will exhaust me," he countered as he joined her at the sink.

"Very well, but afterwards, you really should take a nap." She flashed him a smile as she handed him the plate. "It goes in the cabinet to your left, middle shelf. And the chopsticks go in the drawer right next to you." From the way he looked at them, she could almost read his mind. Unless Jane was mistaken, Max probably lumped Nick and Hannah's New Age life-style in with the dark age of astrology.

"Tell me, how long have your friends been on the Orient Express?" he asked, confirming her suspicions.

"About ten years," Jane replied carefully. "But before you go jumping the gun—"

"Who said anything about jumping the gun?"

"Considering your opinion of astrology, I can just imagine what you think of acupuncture and wearing kimonos." Gingerly she fingered the one she wore.

"Umm-hmm. And taking off your shoes before coming in the house and sleeping on the floor, just to name a few." He began vigorously drying the glass she handed him. "But you know, as wacky as all this is, I'm actually enjoying myself."

"You are?"

"Oh, didn't you know I was a late-blooming flower child?"

"You were?" With a snap, Jane closed her mouth. "You were not!" Placing another wet glass in his hand, she turned her attention to the frying pan. "Just don't confuse Hannah and Nick with middle-aged hippies. They don't even smoke cigarettes, much less anything else. In fact, Nick volunteers time at the drug-rehab center downtown."

"Hey, don't get so defensive," Max said, then putting the glass to one side, he hooked the tea towel around Jane's neck and drew her toward him. Instantly, her heart began pounding, and throwing her hands against his rock-hard chest, she tried to stem the thrill of pleasure that fluttered inside of her.

"You've...you've had a blow to the head," she managed to say. "And you're probably not yourself."

"Then who the hell am I? Napoleon?" Easing the tension on the towel, he slowly released her. The gleam was definitely back in his eye.

"As I was saying," she began, grasping at straws, "you should really rest."

"While *The Alexandrian* runs itself?"

"Yes." Her voice was much steadier, thank God. They were on good old professional ground. With precise movements, she wrung out the dish rag and began a pointless and repetitious buffing of the steel drain board. Max's large hand closed over hers, and she felt every muscle in her body tense.

"There's something you're not telling me, Jane." The pressure on her hand increased as he slowly moved closer.

"If you're talking about last night, I guess you're right." Pulling away from him, she turned toward the window, only to find herself spun around and staring into his eyes. "I promise I'll tell you this afternoon, but only if you do as Nicky said." She swallowed hard, and wondered if he could hear her heart beat.

"It must have been quite an evening," he murmured. "Just what did happen before I got my lights knocked out?" For one heart-stopping moment, it seemed to Jane as if he might kiss her. His blue-eyed gaze went right through her, and his chest rose and fell rapidly. It was all she could do to keep from collapsing against him. She felt the whisper of his breath against her cheek as his mouth slowly lowered toward hers.

Pluto's fierce bark of alarm broke the spell.

"What the devil..." Max stiffened. Releasing Jane, he quickly stepped back.

"We have company," he muttered over his shoulder as he turned and strode down the hall toward the front door.

"So we do," Jane echoed. Saved by the bell once again, she mused hurrying after Max.

Both dogs were howling at the door, several cats were hissing, and even the parrot had joined in.

The place was a damn circus, Max thought brushing past the mannequins. He yanked open the door.

He didn't know who to expect at that hour of the morning, but it certainly wasn't Rufus, nor was it the petite blonde at his side.

Chapter Five

"Sherry! Rufus!" Jane stepped past Max. "I—I didn't know you knew each other."

"Actually, we don't," Rufus said, shifting his brief-case to his left hand and thrusting out his right. "But I gather you're Sherry Devine, so it's a pleasure to meet you. Rufus Quinton's the name, investigative reporter for *The Alexandrian*."

"Come on in, before the menagerie escapes," Jane said as she scooped up a black cat, then with her foot she deflected the yellow tabby. Stepping to one side, she made quick introductions.

Max was brimming with questions, but Jane who led them into the living room and practically shoved Rufus and him onto a futon couch, hooked arms with Sherry Devine and mumbling something about fixing tea, dis-appeared into the kitchen.

"I hope it's not that tea you gave me at breakfast," Max called after her as the yellow cat leapt onto his lap.

Then turning to Rufus he added, "Welcome to *The Twilight Zone.*"

"What on earth happened to you?"

"Didn't Jane tell you?"

"She said you'd had an accident and wouldn't be in the office today. When I tried to find out more, she gave me this address and said to stop by before going to work. She promised to fill me in."

"Don't count on it. I have a feeling Jane is pretty good at making long-range promises."

"You know Max, you don't look so good."

"I've felt better. However, considering—"

"Have you seen a doctor?"

"In a manner of speaking. But considering everything—" he tapped the bandage on his head "—I'm pretty lucky that I don't have total amnesia."

"What do you mean, 'amnesia'?"

"Memory loss."

"I know what it means." Rufus removed his glasses and quickly buffed the lenses, then holding them up to the light for inspection he carefully said, "So, you're saying you've forgotten something."

"An entire evening," Max replied somewhat cheerfully, watching as the yellow cat shifted his allegiance to Rufus's lap. "I'm told I have a concussion, but can't remember how or where it happened. However, since then I've been acupunctured, compressed, given suspicious-looking teas to drink and been surrounded by all this—" his broad sweep of the hand was intended to indicate more than just the living room "—it's kind of like shock therapy. But enough of that. Now that you're here, perhaps you can tell me just what the devil I had on my calendar last night." With a grunt, he rose to his feet. "Don't tell me to sit down or I'll..." Feeling a wave of dizziness, Max took a deep breath and crossing to the mantel, propped himself against it.

"You look like a drunk trying to navigate a straight line in the hoosegow," Rufus remarked as he gingerly got to his feet, and with the purring cat tucked under his arm, joined his friend. "Okay, my turn to play doctor. Do you remember our installing the new equipment last night?"

"Yes. Everything's reasonably clear up until then. After that though, I think I blew a few brain cells." He paused to rub some of the tension from his shoulders. "The next thing I remember, Jane was waking me up and I thought we were back at the paper and that the lights had gone out. Things got a little fuzzy after that. I sort of went from blown fuse to having needles stuck in me. So, fill me in."

"You asked—no, take that back—you told me to be Jane's bodyguard—"

"Oh, yes! I *do* remember that. In fact I went to sleep wondering where in the blue blazes you were last night."

"I figured when you dropped Jane off after dinner, that was that. Was I supposed to camp outside her door all night?" Rufus asked as he deposited the now-squirming cat onto the mantel.

"No, no, of course not," Max replied, shoving his hands into the kimono's pockets. "It would be a big help though, if you told me where we had dinner. Don't look at me like that. I'm not kidding about this memory business."

"The Water View Inn. Ring any bells?"

"Go on," Max urged as he began to pace in front of the fireplace.

"You and Jane went into the main panorama room, and I ducked into the oyster bar. By the way, if I never see another oyster or shrimp, it won't be too soon. Got that old boy?''

"Water View Inn . . .'' Max paused midstride beneath the poster of George Harrison and let out a sigh. "No bells yet. But go on.''

"Since we didn't have walkie-talkies, I'm afraid I can't give you a blow-by-blow account of your evening. Although it lasted long enough, and if—''

"I know, I know. If you never see another oyster or shrimp, etcetera, etcetera. So what did Jane and I do afterwards?''

"I was getting to that, old boy. You and Jane took a stroll down the pier. Again, I wasn't close enough to take it down verbatim, but—''

"Ha. Some investigative reporter you make!'' Max said on a laugh.

"I haven't stooped to the *Weekly Intruder*'s tactics yet. However, I had a pretty good view, and from the looks of it—'' Rufus gave his friend a wink "—I'd say you're missing a *very nice* memory.''

"*That* good?'' Absently Max stroked the yellow cat.

"It wasn't *From Here to Eternity,* but for a first whatever it was you were having, it looked promising.''

"Damn! How long did I stay in her apartment?''

"You didn't go inside.''

"I didn't?''

"You didn't. You shook hands at the door. Very proper. Although, if I didn't know better, I'd wonder at last night's arrangements.'' With a gesture toward Max's kimono, Rufus added, "You and Jane look very comfortable in your *Mikado* sleepwear.''

"Save speculation for your column. Right now I want to know what else I might have done last night.''

Rufus looked blankly at his friend for a moment, then on a long exhale, he said, "Come to think of it, you did mention checking out Dr. Zodiac. Said you were going to do it after dinner"

"That's right. . . . I remember that I'd planned to do that."

"Hey, wait a minute. Don't tell me I was supposed to follow you, too."

"As it happens, it might have been a help. Then again, you might have been knocked out, too. But do me a favor—"

"I know. Keep tabs on Miss Smith. I gather you don't want the office to know anything about this."

"Ha! What's there to know?" Max asked, not really addressing Rufus. Then, leaning against the mantel, he closed his eyes for a second in hope that the dizziness would pass.

"Max!" At the sound of Jane's voice, Max jerked his head up, and immediately regretted the sudden movement as a sharp pain shot through his skull.

"Are you all right?" she asked, hurrying over to his side and hooking her arm through his.

"I'm not going to keel over, if that's what you mean," Max replied, thoroughly annoyed with his weakness. Then, noticing that she and Sherry had their coats on, he said, "What are you all up too?"

"Sherry and Rufus are going to stop by my office for some coffee, and then I'm going to write my column. And you, dear boss, are going to rest. Doctor's orders, remember?"

"I wish I did," he quipped. "Remember, that is. You see, I'm still in the dark about last night. By the way and I hope I'm not being too nosy, but why is Miss Devine here?"

"Camilla, at the paper, told her she could find me here. I'll answer the rest of your questions this afternoon," Jane promised in a voice that reminded Max of his fifth-grade teacher.

She was going to have a lot to answer for later. He wasn't quite sure what he was going to do to her, but feeling her softness innocently pressed against his arm was rekindling some old ideas.

"I've made some fresh camomile tea, and despite what you think you really do need your sleep." Having left Sherry and Rufus in the living room, Jane had managed to herd Max into the guest room as she spoke. "Pluto and Toto will keep you company, and I'll be back midafternoon." She pressed her index finger to his lips, and it was all Max could do to keep from nibbling it. "Shh now, no arguing."

The light floral scent she wore made him want to nibble her.

"You're to drink the tea and go to bed," she reminded him with a devilish smile.

"You're going to pay for this," he teased.

"Right! Something about the cure killing the patient?" Without waiting for his reply, she headed for the door. "Don't worry about a thing. Rufus will see that things run smoothly at the paper, and your secretary can handle any loose ends that come up. Don't worry!" She blew him a kiss and rejoined Sherry and Rufus.

Stretching out on the futon and crossing his arms behind his head, Max stared at the ceiling and for the hundredth time wondered what he'd done the night before. At least now he knew it was in connection with Astroscope. Maybe he'd gone over to their headquarters and...what? Gotten brained for trespassing? Great, just great! He'd issued Jane all sorts of warnings, and what happens? *She* rescues *him*.

This did not sit well with Max. He belonged behind his desk at *The Alexandrian,* not lounging about drinking teas and staring at ceilings. He reached for the lukewarm tea and drank it as quickly as possible. Maybe a little sleep wouldn't hurt, he decided on an unexpected yawn. Funny, he'd thought this ceiling had clouds painted on it, too.

A scratching sound roused Max and jerking forward, he came eye to eye with Pluto, who gave him a lick on the face before collapsing onto his paws. Toto, followed in turn by the yellow cat, was right behind him. A curious trio, if Max had ever seen one. Strangely enough, it gave him the oddest sense of family.

Reluctantly, Max closed his eyes. His head felt better, but despite his grumblings to the contrary, he really was pretty beat.

Jane, somewhat taken aback by Sherry's impromptu visit, was thankful to have clued her in before Max had a chance to grill the dancer about Dr. Zodiac. And from the look on his face, he had seemed about to do just that. Jane knew she owed him an explanation, but if he was reminded of her pending appointment with Dr. Z., she knew all hell would break out. Even Rufus, after being apprised of the situation, agreed with her tactics. Both he and Sherry were quite pleased that she'd managed to photograph Astroscope's props.

"By the way," Jane continued as she waited for her computer to warm up, "thanks a lot for bringing my gloves by. I couldn't imagine where I'd left them."

"Well, it's supposed to be cold and windy today, so I figured you'd need them," Sherry said. "You might even want to keep them on for your interview. Dr. Z. keeps the place as cold as a morgue! He claims the spirits like it that way.''

Sherry smiled above the steaming cup of coffee she'd been sipping. She and Rufus were sitting on the tiny loveseat parallel to Jane's desk. They held their coffee cups at precisely the same angle, and unless Jane was mistaken, she had inadvertently brought together quite an incongruous pair of love birds.

"Well, I don't want to keep you from your column," Sherry said, "but I am enjoying our visit." Shaking her head she added, "Only wish I'd known about *you* before hocking my soul to Astroscope."

"But then Dr. Zodiac's scam wouldn't have come to our attention," Jane replied as she typed the date into her computer.

"True enough." Sherry stood up and after an awkward silence said, "It was good meeting you, Rufus. I hope we run into each other again."

As Jane looked up at the pair, she smiled to herself. She'd have to take an especially close look at the planet Venus today. Maybe it even deserved being highlighted in her column.

"Well ladies, how about lunch, then? Say around twelve-thirty?"

"I'd love to," Sherry answered before Jane had time to recover from Rufus's invitation.

"What do you say, Janey?"

"I'm going to have to decline, Rufus. I'm almost two hours behind schedule. Now, don't look at me like that. You know how it is when *you're* behind." She winked at him, and was pleasantly surprised by an uncharacteristic wink back.

"We want a full report when you return from your assignation with Dr. Z.," Rufus warned as he and Sherry headed for the door.

"*Assignation?* Spare me!"

"All the details," he reiterated.

"Just so long as you keep all this under your hat, Mr. Quinton. In other words, let *me* handle Max."

"With kid gloves," Rufus promised. "But please, no more monkeying around in dark storehouses, okay?"

"Right," Jane said, mentally crossing her fingers as she turned back to her computer. It was almost eleven o'clock. Normally she would have printed out the day's astrology wheel and been halfway through her column by now. Then of course, there was the mail, which she probably wouldn't even get to until tomorrow. And with an average of twenty queries a day, she would have to increase her other column, "Just Ask Greta," to three times a week to handle the volume. However, this was not the time to bring that up with Max.

Max. She lifted her fingers off the keys and leaning forward, stared at the day's wheel. She had to get her mind off of Max and onto the column. She'd already not only done his chart, but had compared his chart to hers and had made a chart for their relationship. According to the stars, it was blessed six ways to Sunday. Jane almost wished she hadn't punched it up. It was practically a text-book blueprint for a sparks-flying, no-holds-barred relationship. Why had she done it?

"Because I'm a nut, that's why!" Jane announced to the screen.

She then pressed the Print key and waited while the companion machine, which reminded her of a giant sugar cube, spat out a paper copy of the wheel. Mercury in Aries was about to make a humdinger of an aspect with Jupiter. Good Lord, Max would be in his glory. The prospect was just a bit much.

A short while later, Jane stood before the receptionist at Astroscope. The woman vaguely reminded her of the wicked but beautiful queen in *Snow White*. She was long, svelte and wore her blue-black hair swooped into a tight French roll. In what could have been a Transylvanian accent, she told Jane to have a seat, that "the professor" would see her shortly. Then pursing her ruby lips into a smile, the woman continued typing, an amazing feat, considering the glittery talons at the tips of her fingers.

It was all Jane could do to keep from staring at the woman. Seated behind a black-lacquered desk, dressed in a black velvet caftan, the receptionist seemed about to melt into the black carpet, or perhaps into the mirrored walls. Glancing at the ceiling Jane noticed it too, was now black—a change from her first visit, when it had been sky blue. Running her hands across the purple velvet of the couch on which she was sitting, Jane wondered who had decorated the place.

Idly she picked up a copy of *The Purple Petal* and was leafing through it in search of further testimonials when the front door opened and a blue-haired little old lady, dripping in diamonds, fox furs and restraining a yappy French poodle, approached the front desk. She was obviously a welcome client, perhaps arriving for her monthly checkup, for the wicked queen actually rose to greet her. Undoubtedly the diamonds were very real.

Suddenly at the sound of chimes another woman, probably Dr. Z.'s secretary, entered from a side door. She resembled the receptionist, only she was shorter and with her hair, straight and blunt cut, she reminded Jane of a comic book character. With a nod in Jane's direction, she ushered her into what could only be described as the inner sanctum. How Jane had missed this gem last visit, she'd never know.

"Please enter, Miss Starr." A heavily accented voice, which echoed in the high-ceilinged chamber, caused Jane to jump and practically stumble forward over what seemed like an ocean of pale lavender carpet. For an idiotic moment she felt a little like Dorothy approaching the Wizard of Oz. The walls and ceilings of Dr. Zodiac's chamber were covered with tinted mirrors, the kind one usually sees in posh bathrooms. The "professor" was seated behind what looked like a marble desk with the signs of the zodiac stamped in gold around its rim. Jane took a deep breath of the incensed air, then slowly came forward.

"It is a pleasure indeed, to see you again." The faintest hint of a smile tugged at his features. Jane couldn't help but imagine him torturing nonbelievers in some underground passage.

"I'm surprised you remember me after six months," Jane said with what she hoped was just the right touch of modesty.

"Like your name Miss Starr, you are destined to burn brightly. And I hasten to add, your luminosity has not been forgotten." With a twirling gesture he indicated her hair, then with another flourish he added, "Please have a seat, my destiny."

His destiny? Whatever destiny they shared, she would very much like to avoid it. Dr. Z. was exactly the kind of astrologer that gave the profession bad press; he was the epitome of what Max had made fun of the other night. Settling into the indicated seat, a dark rococo monstrosity with purple velvet cushions, Jane smiled expectantly at Dr. Zodiac, who returned the smile with considerable interest.

"Business before pleasure," he intoned, looking at her from hooded eyes. "I've been looking over your application from last September, and I only repeat myself when I say you would be a definite addition to our staff. Your experience is a real plus." As he lifted his dark eyes from the application, Jane felt them practically bore holes through her. Maybe he wasn't accustomed to redheads, she told herself. And maybe he was a lech.

Jane steadied her smile. "I'm glad you find me qualified."

"Qualified?" Zodiac leaned back and let out a bark of laughter. "You're more than qualified, Miss Starr. And I've checked some of your references." Steepling his fingers he slowly added, "Though I seem to forget why you left sunny California and all those lovely clients."

"I got tired of the endless summer," she replied candidly, doing her best to remember her trumped-up résumé. "Although quite frankly, I'd hoped to sort of trade movie stars for politicians, but the going's been slower than I'd anticipated."

"Now that you're becoming part of the Astroscope family, I promise you all that will change. Many of our clients are in high places. And for you Miss Starr, may I say that the sky's the limit." Fingering her application, Dr. Z. gave her a look that could melt wax.

"Then I'm ready for takeoff," Jane said on a burst of genuine excitement.

"Would tomorrow be too soon?" Zodiac asked, rising to an impressive height and slowly circling to the front of his desk.

"Just point me in the right direction." She was practically levitating off her chair.

"I've got a new client who's worried about some dreams she's been having about her deceased husband. Wouldn't tell me too much about them. Said she wants to confide in a woman astrologer. And would you believe, my dear Miss Starr, that you fill the bill?"

"Oh?"

"Yes. She said she dreamed she would be a tall redhead. Please stand, Miss Starr." Zodiac had lowered his voice, and reaching for Jane's hand, he pulled her to her feet. "You are the one," he murmured with a sudden reverence that gave Jane goose bumps. "Later I will tell you about our past lives together. But for now, I will get the charts and information my assistant has prepared. I shall return." His glance moved over her, and Jane could have sworn he was about to click his heels and kiss her hand.

The moment he left the room, she hurried around his desk and although unsure just what she hoped to find, yanked open several drawers until she spotted a stack of eight-by-ten glossy photos of Dr. Z. Although she could undoubtedly have gotten one simply by asking, it would be better if he didn't know she had it, especially since it was going to appear on the front page of *The Alexandrian*. Alerted by a sound from the hall, she scooted around to the front of the desk just as Dr. Zodiac entered. Her heart was going like a bell clapper, and she was breathing as if she'd just crossed a finish line.

Thankfully Dr. Z. was too preoccupied to notice. "I am most distressed that my assistant has not yet prepared the charts. I'll call you later this evening when they're ready, if that's all right."

"Sure. No problem," Jane replied in a breathless voice. "I gather my client is in the area?" Even though her cheeks were burning with incriminating color, she flashed him a smile and managed to hold her ground.

As Dr. Zodiac moved toward her, she felt a ripple of apprehension. Dressed in deep purple with chunky gold chains around his neck, he was definitely imposing. Jane seriously doubted if her best karate kick would so much as make a dent in the man's armor.

"I suppose you can give me the address later," she offered smoothly, countering his move with one of her own toward the door.

"Yes. Later," he murmured. "There is much we need to discuss—"

"About my client," Jane put in hopefully as she took another step toward the door. "And of course about Astroscope's policies and long range goals—where the client is concerned." Her hand connected with the door knob.

"In your deepest being you already know. For together, we have shared many memories, Amber Starr." As his icy fingers closed around hers, Jane felt she'd just been put into deep freeze. "Tomorrow night I will reveal those things you've forgotten."

"I—I've got an engagement," she said a trifle too quickly, "but what about the next night."

"Thursday night it is," he confirmed with a flash of teeth that reminded Jane of tombstones.

"That—that...sounds great," she replied, stepping back as Dr. Zodiac opened the door for her. "Why don't we meet at—at...The Pisces Moon Pub," she added energetically. No one she knew would see her there, especially not Max.

"Indeed," Dr. Z. muttered, clasping her hand to his lips. "Shall we say seven-thirty?"

Jane gave him her melt-down smile and said, "Seven-thirty it is!"

Chapter Six

Jane's elation peaked at the corner of Braddock Road and Mount Vernon Avenue. She had been giddy with her success since sailing out of the Astroscope offices, and it was all she could do to keep from running red lights on her way back to Hannah's. She'd report in to Rufus after she got Max situated.

Max. How on earth was she going to deal with him? Hit him over the head again? Pray that his amnesia continued until she'd finished? No, of course not! Everything was going to work out fine. After all, it was a glorious day filled with sunshine and bright blue skies. What could possibly go wrong?

Coming to a stop light, Jane felt some of her enthusiasm wane. Just what was she going to tell Max? The whole truth and nothing but the truth, so help her God?

As the light changed to green, Jane's spirits flagged. One more block to go, so she'd better think of something to tell him. Lying wasn't her forte however, she did

PLAY THE "LUCKY 7" SLOT MACHINE GAME !

NO COST! NO OBLIGATION TO BUY! NO PURCHASE NECESSARY!

PLAY "LUCKY 7"
AND GET AS MANY AS SIX FREE GIFTS...

HOW TO PLAY:

1. With a coin, carefully scratch off the silver box at the right. This makes you eligible to receive one or more free books, and possibly other gifts, depending on what is revealed beneath the scratch-off area.

2. You'll receive brand-new Silhouette Romance™ novels. When you return this card, we'll send you the books and gifts you qualify for *absolutely free*!

3. If we don't hear from you, every month we'll send you 6 additional novels to read and enjoy. You can return them and owe nothing but if you decide to keep them, you'll pay only $2.25* per book, and there is *no* extra charge for postage and handling. There are no hidden extras.

4. When you join the Silhouette Reader Service™, you'll get our monthly newsletter, as well as additional free gifts from time to time just for being a subscriber.

5. You must be completely satisfied. You may cancel at any time simply by sending us a note or a shipping statement marked "cancel" or returning any shipment to us at our cost.

*Terms and prices subject to change.
 Sales tax applicable in N.Y.
© 1991 HARLEQUIN ENTERPRISES LIMITED

This lovely Victorian pewter-finish miniature is perfect for displaying a treasured photograph. And it's yours FREE as added thanks for giving our Reader Service a try!

DETACH AND MAIL CARD TODAY

BUSINESS REPLY MAIL
FIRST CLASS MAIL   PERMIT NO. 717   BUFFALO, NY

POSTAGE WILL BE PAID BY ADDRESSEE

SILHOUETTE READER SERVICE
3010 WALDEN AVE
PO BOX 1867
BUFFALO NY 14240-9952

NO POSTAGE
NECESSARY
IF MAILED
IN THE
UNITED STATES

fairly well when it came to exaggeration. Surely she was capable of handling Max.

Turning onto Hannah's street, Jane refused to think about his other attributes. After all, lots of men were handsome, sexy and successful. So what if he'd almost kissed her...twice. So what if thinking about him made her feel as though she were sixteen and having her first crush. So what! She couldn't think about that now. She had a story to write, and nothing was going to stop her.

Stand your ground Janey, she silently counseled herself as she parked the car. Of all the signs, only Pisces could worry themselves to death. If she'd been born Aries or Sagittarius, she wouldn't spend five minutes on this type of nonsense.

The wind, which had picked up considerably, gave her all the incentive she needed to dash from the car to the house. Seeing Max standing in the doorway however, brought her up short. His smile was positively Machiavellian.

"Welcome, Ms. Smith.... It *is* Smith on Tuesdays, isn't it?"

"Sure," she replied after a beat. Then, averting her gaze, she crouched down and greeted her dogs. Somehow she had to keep Max from pressing her about Dr. Z. "So, what have you been up to?"

"Reading a book on ESP."

Straightening, she looked him in the eye. "ESP?" Patting Pluto on the head, she entered the house, quickly shed her coat and started for the kitchen.

"Yes. ESP," Max replied, following her down the hall. "You know, extrasensory perception?"

"Somehow I wouldn't have thought that up your alley. You must be feeling better." Dropping her purse onto a stool, she headed for the refrigerator. "Cream-of-carrot soup sound good to you?"

"Sounds fine. Yes, I'm feeling much better, thank you." Joining her by the refrigerator door, he added, "ESP is *not* up my alley, but the choice was limited to reading that or a vegetarian cookbook."

Jane shot him a withering look. "Max, you're exaggerating. But you do look better." Thrusting her hand into the vegetable tray, she pulled out a head of lettuce, some scallions and a bag of mushrooms. "How about a salad?"

"I'll do it," he said, relieving her of the makings.

"Oh, you sure?"

"Men make the best chefs, haven't you ever heard that?" He smiled at her from the sink. "How about some red pepper?"

"My, my! We *are* in top form. Maybe you should get knocked unconscious more often." Brushing past him, she deposited a shiny red pepper in the colander.

"Are you volunteering for the job?" he asked, giving the lettuce a quick rinse.

"Manual labor isn't my thing," she answered sweetly, stirring the soup. "Besides, I long ago gave up trying to knock sense into men." Even with her back to Max, Jane thought his gaze was almost as hot as the burner in front of her. "Any memories?" she inquired on a purposefully light note as she continued stirring the pot.

"I'm working on it."

"They'll come back."

"A little help from you wouldn't hurt," Max said to her as he began chopping vegetables. "You know my twelve-hour observation period is up. I haven't frothed at the mouth, bitten you or—"

"We're talking concussion, Max, not rabies."

"Thanks for reminding me. You know how it is with these memory lapses."

"I'm not exactly an expert." She turned the soup off and ladeled it into bowls.

"You studied Oriental medicine," he protested.

"That's different. Besides, I wasn't making a career of it. Salad almost ready?"

"Well, some ham and cheese would help. But I suppose that would be like asking for hamburgers in India."

"Bingo." On her way to the table, Jane peered at the salad. "An admirable job, considering the dearth of material you had to work with. But then, a true artist can create with anything."

"It's not the same as the salmon steak and baked potatoes I dreamed about this morning."

"Salmon steak?" Jane blinked up at him. "That's a coincidence, I was thinking about picking some up for dinner." Seeing the expectant grin on his battle-worn face she laughed and said, "Okay Max, you're on. But stand forewarned, you'll have K.P. duty afterwards."

"Oh, but nurse, I was wounded in the line of duty, and I still haven't regained my memory. Are you sure—"

"Positive, buster. You forget, it takes time to get your memory back."

"That's just my problem, I *have* forgotten."

"Eat your soup," she said laughing. "Carrots are good for the brain."

"Don't you mean good for the eyes?"

"Whatever. And the green stuff you're poking at is watercress."

"Oh, and I suppose that's good for my triple heater." He sent her an amused glance. "You see, I do remember some things." Watching her carefully for a response, Max bet his bottom dollar she was holding something back, but until he could remember what the dickens they'd done last night, he was shooting in the dark.

After lunch that Jane mandated Max rest while she returned to the office. But Max had very different ideas. He had a newspaper to get out, a desk full of work and a Tuesday-afternoon staff meeting, not to mention his editorial to write.

"Well then, at least let me drive you," Jane offered, stumbling after him in his flight to the door. She had her coat half on and half off, and was clutching her open pocketbook, while trying to navigate around various small animals that cluttered the path.

"I don't need a chauffeur yet," Max assured her over his shoulder. "Let's hope I'll remember who I am long enough to get to work." Reaching the door, he spun around just as she slammed into him. "We've got to stop meeting like this," he murmured, all too aware of the distracting effect she was having on him. "What will the neighbors say?"

"I wouldn't know!" she exclaimed, jumping back as if he were a hot poker. "But I still say you're not in any condition to be driving all over town."

"You could come with me to make sure I get there," he interrupted. He couldn't remember seeing her look this good. Perhaps, he thought wryly it was because he couldn't remember period. "Well?" he prodded.

"I'll follow you in my car," Jane answered, thrusting her other arm into the coat. "I've got a few things to do at the paper too, you know." With a toss of her head, she preceded Max out the door, then after giving a sharp whistle for her dogs, started toward her car.

"You bringing them to the office, too?" Max called after her.

"Why not," she said cheerily as she ushered the dogs into the back seat. "Mascots for *The Alexandrian*. We'll have to bring that up at the meeting this afternoon."

Max gave her a wave as he headed for his car, only to pause in front of it. "Hey, how did my car get here anyway?"

"I drove it," Jane replied, jumping into the front seat of her own vehicle. Then rolling down the window, she gave Max a smile that went right through him. "And you're right, it does drive like a dream."

"But nothing to compare with your old Blue Gem, right?" Climbing behind the wheel of his car, he called over to her. "I take it you realize I'm capable of navigating the distance to the paper unescorted."

"Nevertheless, we'll be right behind you. Once you're safely inside, I'll drop the dogs off at my place. I need to change anyway."

"This is wacky. I don't care if we are in the nineties, the man is supposed to be the one who sees the lady to her door. What you need is—"

"You Tarzan, me Jane, right?" Her voice was maddeningly chipper, as if she thrived on driving Max nuts.

"You're being ridiculous. I'm not Tarzan, and you're—"

"Not Jane?" With an impish smile she said, "That's right. On Tuesdays I'm Amber. Now drive on, Maxwell Cornelius."

Maxwell Cornelius? Good Lord, no one called him that and lived.

Max brooded off and on throughout the afternoon, and though he tried to play down the incident with his employees, it was still quite literally a sore point. Right before the weekly meeting, the staff filed into his office, bearing gifts: Midge the culinary editor, brought pastries; Harry from arts and entertainment, a video; Roy the sports editor, a baseball bat signed by members of the New York Yankees; and Camilla the society editor, a box of Godiva chocolates. The rest of the staff had gone in on an enormous bouquet. By the time Rufus and Jane showed up with a singing balloon man and several bottles of sparkling cider, it was obvious that the weekly meeting would be postponed a day.

"You're late," Max said from his seated position on his desk. "But thanks for the balloons."

"They're to lift your spirits," Jane informed him, reaching for a chocolate.

"I thought you eschewed such indulgences, especially after that hearty lunch!"

"I've been known to partake." Biting into a raspberry cordial, she let out a sigh. "Moderation in all things." Then joining Max on the edge of the desk, she said, "Well, what do you think of our little shindig?"

"Let's have one a month—great for group morale. Did you get that Camilla?"

A willowy blue-eyed blonde, who was pretending fascination at something the sports editor was saying, swiveled her lovely neck in Max's direction. "Did I get what, darling?"

"That we should have a party a month." With a laugh he added, "Of course, when I get my memory back, I'll deny all of this."

"Sweet Max," she crooned, "it's going on the social calendar, so you can't forget!"

"Absolutely!" Midge chimed in. "All work and no fun makes Max a dull boy. Perhaps I can even get a local restaurant to cater it."

"Me and my big mouth," Max groaned.

"Not at all," Midge protested as she eased her considerable girth onto Max's desk. "I think it's a fabulous idea. Don't you, Jane?"

"Absolutely," she replied with a grin. "See you all in a bit."

Before Max could counter this, she had slipped off her perch and was halfway across the room. Try as he might, the culinary editor had him cornered, and from his two-weeks' experience at the paper, he knew that once started, the woman would expound on French cooking the way a philosopher might go into Plato. Idly he wondered what she'd think of Hannah's pristine stockpile of grains and legumes.

On the other side of the room, Jane bit back a smile. She probably shouldn't have abandoned Max, but this was the only opportunity she'd have to try to reach Hannah.

"You're not leaving, are you?" Rufus stopped her, bobbing a balloon in her direction.

"Only long enough to touch base with Hannah."

"You mean you haven't told her you're going to be her astrologer?"

"Shh!" Jane sidled up to him. "Do you want everyone to know?"

"If you mean Max, he's going to have to be told sooner or later."

"Just the same, I'll opt for later." She smiled again and slipped out the door.

On reaching her office, Jane breathed a sigh of relief. What was it with Rufus, anyway? All afternoon he'd been glued to her like a shadow. On top of that, he'd practically given her the third degree.

Picking up the phone, she punched in the Happy Harvest number and was relieved to hear Hannah's voice after the third ring.

"We've hit the jackpot, Ms. Ritchie," Jane announced as she plopped onto her chair.

"Amber Starr, I presume?" On a hoot of laughter, Hannah said, "Dr. Zodiac's assistant just called to tell me. Would you believe tomorrow at four o'clock? Hey, you won't have any trouble with Max, will you?"

"I'm not planning on it," Jane rejoined. "By the way, thanks for everything last night. Max really has made a remarkable recovery."

"Memory, too?"

"Well, not yet. In a way it's a blessing because at least he's not going on about Dr. Z."

"And when his memory comes back?"

"I'd rather not think of all the nasty names he's going to call me then." Coiling the telephone cord around her hand, she added, "After all, it's not my fault he got hit on the head. I mean, if he'd taken me into his confidence, probably none of that would have happened. Anyway, Max is blissfully in the dark."

"Until he has sudden recall," Hannah reminded her with a laugh. "By the way, Sherry stopped by a while ago. She wanted to know what the story was with Rufus. Well, since I'd only met him once, I didn't know what to say, but I told her he was an okay guy. Seems they'd had a cozy lunch, with hints of even more coziness to come." Hannah paused.

"I figured as much. So what happened?"

"You knew about this?"

"Yeah. Go on."

"Guess you saw it in the stars."

"More like in their eyes. For Pete's sake, tell me what Rufus did."

"During the main course, he asked her out to dinner and dancing, then backed out by the time dessert arrived. Sherry was just wondering if the guy had a history of that sort of thing. Anyway, I thought you might have some pearls of wisdom for her."

"Come to think of it, Rufus has been acting a little strangely. I'll tell you about it tomorrow during our astrology session," Jane said with a laugh. "But for now, I've gotta sign off and get down to the fish market. Max is coming by for dinner."

"Ah-ha!" Hannah murmured.

"Oh, ah-ha, yourself. It's just my good deed for the week, so you can put away your Cupid's bow. See you later tonight. We should be finished with dinner by nine or so."

"I'd hate to interrupt anything—"

"Oh Hannah, for heaven's sake!"

If it hadn't been for a faulty radiator leaking all over her living room floor, Jane might have been ready when Max arrived. As it was, she greeted him with dripping wet hair and dressed in a faded blue-and-white kimono.

"Am I late for dinner, or is this a pajama party?" he asked, clearly amused as he stepped inside. Then shucking off his suede jacket, he sniffed the air. "Smells like you...umm..."

"Burned something? No, I did not." Snatching his jacket from him, she marched over to the closet, mumbling something indistinguishable under her breath.

"We can go out for dinner, if you like. My treat." Following closely behind her, Max took an unexpected delight in the fresh scent of shampoo that drifted toward him. As she whirled to face him, the towel around her hair fell to one side like the Leaning Tower of Pisa.

"Thanks, but dinner *is* under control. Everything else is in chaos, but I promise to feed you, that is if you still have an appetite after all those goodies this afternoon."

"Oh, I'm primed and ready for salmon." And that wasn't all he was hungry for, he thought as he watched her hang up his jacket.

"Good," she said on a cheerier note. "Why don't you make yourself comfy while I change."

"What you've got on is fine with me," Max said, allowing his gaze to sweep the length of her. "Although, if I'd known we were going Oriental, I'd have worn something besides jeans and a crew neck."

"We're not going Oriental, and as you can see, my furniture is strictly Western." Heading toward the stairs, she added, "The living room should be warm by now. What you're smelling is steam from a broken radiator. I had to turn it off." As she reached the top of the stairs, she unwound the towel from around her hair, and leaning over the bannister, called down to him, "Pluto and Toto are still outside. Why don't you let them in."

Max stared absently at the top of the stairs where she had stood. Seeing her with that mass of red hair tumbling about her shoulders had nearly been his undoing.

A sudden howling from the back of the house brought Max back to the present. He supposed the back door was down the hall, but the idea of asking Jane directions seemed ridiculous. After all, even if he didn't remember it, he'd been here last night. Who knows, maybe being here would trigger his memory?

Unfortunately, what he'd hoped would look familiar, merely looked attractive, neat, even artistic. But hardly familiar.

One thing was for sure, the dogs remembered Max only too well. They greeted him as if he were a long-lost friend, and they didn't give him peace until he produced dog biscuits.

"So much for devotion," he muttered good-naturedly as he continued his tour. He estimated the house had been built in the early 1800s, and still had what looked like original flooring and gas light fixtures. The long hall that extended from the kitchen to the front vestibule was filled with old prints, lithographs and several framed citations. On closer inspection, Max discovered they had all been awarded to Randolph Smith for excellence in TV journalism.

"Randolph Smith," he murmured under his breath. Holy cow, it had to be Jane's father. No wonder she was so damn determined. He stepped back a pace, and as he stared at the three awards, he noticed a small framed photo beneath them. It was of three ski-clad figures laughing gaily and squinting into the camera. It had been shot on a ski slope, and it didn't take Max long to recognize Jane or her father; they were both tall and lean with fiery red hair and a determined glint in the eye. The older woman in the photo was undoubtedly Jane's mother.

"Hungry?" Startled by her voice, he stepped back, feeling a bit guilty, as if he'd been caught snooping. One look at Jane though, brought a fresh set of feelings to deal with. The soft light in the hall made her hair sparkle and her eyes glow; she wore a silky jade-green blouse that was loosely belted over a pair of snug jeans. It made him ache just to look at her.

"From the expression on your face, I guess you just discovered who Pops is."

"*Pops?* You call Randolph Smith 'Pops'?"

"Well, he is my father."

"You could have told me..." Realizing how absurd that sounded, he let his words trail off.

"Maybe I already did," she parried as she led the way to the kitchen.

"*Did* you tell me?" he asked, following her to the stove.

He was rewarded by her bubbling laugh. "No, I didn't." Turning around, she slapped a lemon into his hand. "Cut it into quarters. I'll turn on the broiler, and everything else is set—including the table."

"Why is it," he mused, "that we always land in the kitchen?"

"Like at a good party, it's where the action is." Pulling the salad out of the refrigerator, she asked, "Can you think of a better room?"

"Now that you mention it..." He sent her a lazy smile and was gratified by her immediate blush.

"In Oriental medicine they say everything starts in the kitchen," she said, ignoring his comment. Then regarding his technique with the knife, she added somewhat thoughtfully, "You slice lemons well."

"Is there some ancient meaning behind the way one slices lemon?"

"Undoubtedly. Oh, just ignore the dogs," Jane said. "They'll beg for anything. They like to play field hockey with lemons."

"How come you didn't tell me that your father was Randolph Smith?"

"Max, what if he were a plumber? Wouldn't it have been a little strange if I had come up to you that first day on the job and said, 'My father's Randolph Smith, the plumber.'" With a pert nod, she picked up several bowls and headed for the dining room.

"Point made." Max looked down at Toto, who, having given up on the lemon, was again chewing on Max's shoe. "Hey, Jane, I think your dogs are hungry."

"Oh, is Toto eating your foot?" she asked from the dining room.

"Trying to."

"It's just affection," Jane assured him as she reappeared. "They've been fed. Now it's our turn, and if you like, I'll tell you all about Pops." Giving her dog a stern look, she said, "No, Toto!" Then smiling up at Max, she gestured for him to follow her. "You know, ever since I've had Toto, I've gone through shoes faster than stockings."

"That's very *consoling*," Max commented, glancing at his shoe.

Entering the candle-lit dining room, he had the strangest feeling about the evening. And though he couldn't quite put his finger on it, he felt vaguely like a man about to go up the creek without a paddle. There was no doubt about it, odd things happened to him when he got together with Jane Smith.

"I try to eat by candle light twice a week," she explained as she placed a generous portion of salmon steak on his plate. "It makes me happy."

Max nodded in agreement. "It suits you." Then reaching for the wine he added, "May I pour you some?"

"I get first toast," she put in, holding up her fluted glass as he began to pour. When he'd finished, they touched glasses, and she quietly said, "Here's to you regaining your memory."

"Amen." Their eyes met momentarily, then she let her gaze drop, almost as if she were pulling a veil across her lovely candle-lit features. In that single moment, Max felt hopelessly poetic and surprisingly, a little short of breath.

Her eyes flickered up to his again, and it was all he could do to keep from reaching across the table and pulling her into his arms. He was hungry all right, but salmon steaks would only put a small dent in the appetite he'd worked up. Yes, he still knew she was keeping something from him, and though he intended to find out what, he suddenly didn't want to spoil the moment.

After dinner, they adjourned to the living room for coffee. Max, although feeling mellow, was still curious to learn more about Randolph Smith.

"I've been an admirer of your father for many years," he said as he stacked logs in the fireplace. "In fact, back when he had a column in the *Danbury Sun,* he was one of my role models."

"And after he turned to broadcasting?"

"Then, too."

"But what about your own father?" Jane asked, taking a sip of coffee. "Carrying on the family newspaper is no small thing."

"He was my other role model," Max confessed on a laugh. "But it took years before I could admit that to myself. Randolph Smith, on the other hand, was bigger than life, and somehow I could handle that myth better than the nitty-gritty reality of helping my dad run a small-town newspaper." Setting a match to the kindling, he rocked back on his heels and stared at the fire as it crackled to life. On the mantel the clock struck nine. Giving the logs a poke Max added, "When I got out of college, I put as much space as possible between me and *The Alexandrian,* hired on as a stringer for several papers, then finally joined up with the *Dallas Post.* Guess I thought I'd hit the big time. And it was a pretty good paper—''

"Was?" Jane interjected. "The *Post* has always been one of the best in the country."

"They were until last week when the merger went through. They've been given a tabloid window dressing. I suppose I got out while the going was good." He fell silent for a moment, then after giving the fire another poke he added, "There's only a handful of decent papers left in the country."

"Yep. That's what Pops said when he switched over to broadcasting. Not that he thinks television's any better, it simply reaches more people."

Shifting his position by the fire, Max regarded Jane carefully before asking his next question. She was resting back in the loveseat, coffee cup balanced on one knee, a curious expression on her face. "Tell me," he said at last, "was it tough growing up in Pop's shadow?"

"Pops was tops," Jane said simply. "But like you, I didn't really appreciate him until I grew up. Oh, don't get me wrong, I loved him. But he was just...well, Pops. Like other fathers, he had a job, and he was always getting plaques and trophies for it. I grew up thinking that's what adults did. Mom got them for golfing and Pops, for writing." She paused for a sip of coffee, then after a moment added, "Randy—that's my brother—and I sort of traded places. He's the pro golfer, and I'm the writer. Of course, Pops keeps trying to get me into television." Leaning forward, she softly added, "He taught us all

kinds of things—fly fishing, skiing, sailing, canoe-
ing—"

"Astrology?" Max suggested with the merest lift of
an eyebrow.

Jane sniffed audibly, "No, not astrology."

"I didn't think so."

"But he's not against it," Jane quickly added as she
got up and joined Max by the fireplace. "He cham-
pions people's rights to be utter fools if they want."

"Somehow I don't think he considers you anybody's
fool," Max said quietly, turning in time to catch the
surprised expression on her face. "In fact, I'll bet you
take after him."

"Whatever gave you that idea?" she asked as she
picked up the poker and prodded the logs with it.

"Probably something you said or did the other night,
which, unfortunately I can't remember." He watched her
features stiffen.

"Believe me, it's not all that fascinating."

"Oh? I have the feeling, where you're concerned,
things get pretty interesting." Removing the poker from
her hand he added, "You handle this thing like a
weapon."

"Maybe if I hit you over the head, you'd regain your
memory," she teased. "You know, the hair of the dog
that bit you?"

"I'll pass on that, as I'm sure we can find more plea-
surable ways to spend the evening."

"I think our espresso's getting cold," Jane said suddenly as she attempted to get to her feet.

"Let it." Reaching over, he tentatively stroked her
hair. It felt like silk against his palm, its color height-
ened by the firelight. Her face glowed, and her eyes glis-
tened expectantly, as if she'd known this moment was

coming, perhaps was even predestined. Bending closer, Max whispered her name, then drew her to him in a kiss both soft and explosive. He felt her shudder beneath his touch, as longing knifed through him. Deepening the kiss, he heard her sigh of pleasure as she melted against him. Then ever so slowly he felt her arms wrap around him, felt her nails skim along the nape of his neck and felt the yearning for her mount within him as his tongue caressed hers. He'd never known a woman quite like Jane; she could bedevil him one minute and fascinate him the next. But it was more than fascination; he wanted something deeper, more than just this driving feeling that had arisen so quickly between them. Reluctantly he drew back as the powers of reason took over.

"Oh, Janey..." His voice was a husky whisper, and looking into her bright eyes, he felt the longing crest within him once again. He pulled her against his chest and cradled her. There were the sounds of heartbeats, ragged breathing and the ticking clock; nothing more. Words seemed pointless, and yet too much remained unspoken between them: an evening that Max couldn't remember and Jane seemed content to forget.

In fact, Jane suddenly wanted to forget everything except that she was in Max's arms, thrilling to his touch as every nerve ending cried out for more, drinking in his kiss as if she'd never been kissed before. It was a bottomless kiss, rough and raw and urgent. She'd told herself that she wanted to be anywhere but where she was, but she knew now she was wrong.

Where were her hands? Lost somewhere on the rugged terrain of his lean, taut body, tangled in a lock of blond hair, exploring the wonder that was Max Hunter. She felt her body arch in response to his touch as his hands snaked around her back and his lips lowered onto hers yet again.

She met him greedily, eagerly, with a passion and trust that surprised her. Automatically, her hands wrapped around him, drawing him even closer until her breasts, pressed against the nubby cotton of his polo shirt, ached with desire. She heard Max's responding growl, then as he pulled back, saw the heat kindling in his eyes as they raked across her. Slowly, ever so slowly, his mouth descended once again, this time to the pulsating chord at the base of her neck. She wanted this, needed it, craved it . . . and surrendered to it.

"Max. Oh Max," she heard herself murmur as his lips brushed against the fabric of her blouse, his hands seeking out the fullness of her breasts. Then, with a groan, he lowered her onto the rug, his body stretched out beside her. Tenderly, he stroked the curve of her cheek, and it seemed for a moment as if he would take her to him once again, stripping away the layers of protection with which she had insulated herself.

This has to be heaven, Max thought, even as he struggled to dampen the passion that flared like the flames on the hearth. Jane was everything he'd ever dreamed of in a woman, and then some. The maddening part was, he couldn't remember why. All he knew was that she tasted of honey, and her heady fragrance took away his breath, his reason . . . maybe even his memory.

Then again, maybe not. He steadied his breath and pressing his forehead to hers, stared deep into those jewellike eyes as the first glimmer of memory arose. There had been stars above and dark water all around them; they'd been arguing about something, but still he remembered wanting to kiss her, to kiss her and not stop kissing her until she'd gotten some ridiculous idea out of her head. He *had* kissed her...on the forehead.

"Jane?" With an unexpected fierceness, he dragged her against him and took the lips she offered, recklessly plundering their sweetness. One hand eased around to the front of her blouse, then gently slipped between the buttons to the warmth beneath—to where her heart beat like a trapped bird's. How easily he could take her; how vulnerable and open she was to him, and by God, how he wanted her. But feeling her trembled response to his touch brought him back to reality.

"Janey...I..." He pulled back, searching for the words that wouldn't come, yet wanting more than anything else in the world to blot out the distractions that came between them.

The jarring sound of the phone brought Jane to a sitting position.

"They'll call back," Max said, silently cursing the thing for all his frustrations. Clearly though, the mood had been altered.

"You're right," Jane agreed. "Besides, on the third ring my machine gets it." She offered Max a weak smile, then stiffened slightly as the answering machine, set on high volume, filled the air.

"Good evening, Ms. Starr. This is Dr. Zodiac calling to let you know that I've secured your client's chart, and if you would like, you can pick it up tonight. Welcome aboard!" A series of bleeps ended the call and was followed by a silence punctuated only by the tic-tock of the mantel clock.

When Jane finally ventured a look in Max's direction, she knew that at least some of his memory had just returned, and he didn't look one bit amused.

Chapter Seven

"Now, Max, it's not as bad as it sounds," Jane said, scrambling to her feet. "And I was going to tell you everything...eventually." She watched as he slowly got to his feet and moved toward her.

"Eventually?"

"Sure. But I thought that...well, that maybe it would be better if I waited until you were fully recovered."

"My condition didn't seem to bother you a few minutes ago." He cast a disparaging glance toward the hearth rug, whose rumpled appearance gave silent testimony.

"That was different," Jane protested, edging away from him. "This...this—" she waved her hand toward the answering machine "—is business. That was—"

"Pleasure, I'd hoped." His words sounded as if they'd been chipped from ice.

"Yes, yes. It was," she quickly agreed, plastering herself against the wall.

"We aim to please," he pressed, taking another step toward her. But he didn't sound one bit pleased, and from the dangerous glint in his eyes, there was no telling what he'd do. She knew from her research that when Aries men got riled, watch out. And it looked as though she was about to have firsthand experience.

"Maybe we should talk about this," she suggested lamely, "so you can get the whole picture."

"Oh, I think I've just about got the whole picture," Max assured her as he casually propped himself against the wall and gazed down at her. "Let's see if I remember that evening correctly. We had lobster and a rather exceptional white Zinfandel for dinner. We discussed Sherry Devine's soap opera, and you told me you had an appointment with Dr. Zodiac.... Shall I go on?"

"I take it your memory's come back," Jane ventured, wondering just what form his explosion would take. "I'm glad it returned," she added. "You should be too. It was probably Nicky's needles, and then you had a good rest this afternoon, and—"

"Why didn't you just tell me you'd gotten into Astroscope? Did you really think I was going to bite your head off?" With an impatient grunt, he pushed away from the wall. "You could have come to me, trusted me. After all, I *am* your boss."

"I haven't forgotten who you are," she replied, feeling some of her old spunk returning. "And furthermore, I'm not frightened of you even if you are bigger and crazier than I am."

"Crazier than *you?*"

"Yes. At least I don't bully people, threaten to take their jobs away—"

"I don't threaten. I never threaten. I took it away," he said with smug satisfaction. "Then I gave it back."

"Just as bad. Worse!" Jane muttered through clenched teeth as she paced in front of him. "It's misuse of power. And you talk of inspiring trust. How on earth can you expect me to trust you when you're forever issuing ultimatums."

"They were requests for Pete's sake. Hey, could you please stop circling me? You look like some damn lion tamer."

"Oh? I suppose that makes you king of the jungle, doesn't it? Well, I'd better get out my whip."

"Wonderful," Max muttered, throwing his hands up. "And I was fool enough to think that if I got my memory back, we might . . . Oh, never mind." Picking up his untouched espresso, he took a swallow. "Cold."

"Well, what did you expect?" Jane asked without thinking. "What I mean is—"

"I was sure the heat of passion would have kept it at least lukewarm." He stared into the cup for a moment, then carefully placing it back onto the coffee table, he said, "I suppose I didn't know what to expect. Maybe a little honesty."

"No fair! I never lied to you." She could feel every muscle in her body stiffen at the accusation.

"Not out-and-out lying, but—"

"I'm not on trial, and I think this idiotic conversation's gone far enough." She picked up the coffee cups and was headed for the hall when Max stepped in front of her.

"So you're going over to Astroscope. Be reasonable, Jane."

"What I do is my business. After all, I *am* over twenty-one." She tried to push past him, but he wouldn't let her.

"Your age has nothing to do with this. And where this Zodiac freak is concerned, it's my business, as well."

"It might be your business, but it's my life. That is, unless you think you have dominion over that too?"

"By God, woman, you'd drive a saint to sin." As Max stepped away from her Jane made her move, only to be thwarted again. This time, he snatched the cups from her hands and before she could open her mouth, he sealed it with a kiss that knocked the breath out of her. He was breathing hard, and his hands, still tangled in her hair, caressed the nape of her neck. Her own hands were splayed against his chest.

"Do you always take what you want?" she bit out, trying to squelch the traitorous feelings that threatened to surface, trying to ignore the feel of the bristly hairs beneath his shirt.

"When it's offered," he countered huskily. "And unless I'm mistaken—"

"You are!" she said brushing past him. "A minute ago we were fighting, then you start... Oh, I don't know what I mean!"

"I'm trying to be reasonable," he replied, following her into the kitchen.

"That's the second time you've used that word. You're a newspaper man, think of a different one. Besides, it's completely inappropriate where we're concerned." She averted her eyes from what she knew was Max's close scrutiny and began placing dishes into the dishwasher.

"I care about you, damn it all!" he suddenly announced, handing her the detergent.

"If you really cared, you'd let me live my life as I want to, not according to some script you've got in your back pocket. And please don't tell me I'm cute when I'm angry. I've heard that line before." Haphazardly, she dumped the dishwasher detergent into its compartment and slamming the machine closed, flipped the dial and turned it on.

"You're not the cute type," Max said with maddening ease. "And you'll notice I've no script in my back pocket." He made a half turn and slapped himself.

"I hadn't noticed," she lied, quickly untying her apron. "And now, if you don't mind, we'll call it an evening." Good lord, that sounded ridiculous even to her. "I'm glad your memory returned." And that sounded even more absurd, she thought. Taking a deep breath, she turned to face him squarely. "I know you don't approve of my going to pick up the charts from Astroscope, but it's going to look pretty odd if I don't."

"Did Popsie bring you up to be so headstrong?"

"It's Pops, and yes he did. He's an Aquarius, and you know how they are." Whistling for the dogs, she pulled her coat from the hall closet and headed for the door.

"No, I don't know and frankly I don't care how they are. But I can tell you I'm pretty sure Randolph Smith has common sense, a trait obviously not inherited. As for going to Astroscope tonight—"

"Max Hunter, you're not stopping me." Quickly slipping past him, she'd almost made it to the front door before he caught up with her.

"If I told you not to touch a hot stove, you'd probably sit on it, wouldn't you?"

"Dr. Zodiac is not exactly a hot stove," Jane said, shrugging him off. "No more ultimatums, Maxwell Cornelius!"

"Damn it, woman—"

"My name's *Jane*—"

"And I'm *Max*—"

"And I'm going! Period." Puckering her lips, she made an ear-splitting whistle, clapped her hands and shouted, "Pluto! Max treat!"

"What the devil..." Max felt something tug on his pant leg. It was Pluto. "Jane! Get your dog off me!"

"He loves you," she called back gaily as she ran down the walk and jumped into the car. "So does Toto."

"You're out of your mind!" He was shouting at the woman, and all she was doing was waving back at him like Miss America! "You need a keeper more than your dogs do, did anyone ever tell you that?"

"Pops has for years!" Blowing him a kiss she added, "Pluto, Max treat!" and drove off.

"Max treat" must have been the magic words, for immediately, the German shepherd released Max's leg only to jump him from behind and squash him flat to the floor. "Max treat?" Was he about to become Pluto's after dinner munchie? Max wondered.

As if reading his mind the dog gave Max's neck a sniff, then began methodically washing it. Toto, obviously delighted with their captive treasure, stationed himself at Max's feet and started giving his loafers a thorough chewing.

He would kill the woman, Max thought.

No, that was too good for her. Perhaps he could make her cover an antiastrology convention or a fur-trappers conference. He would do something. Craning his neck to the other side, he was rewarded with another wet kiss and what sounded like a growl.

"Friend," he muttered into the carpet. The dog had to weigh a ton. He could just see the banner headline at the *Dallas Post,* "Ex-editor squashed to death by giant German shepherd." As a test, he moved his foot and elicited a sharp yap-yap of disapproval from Toto.

Somewhere, Max remembered hearing that it could be dangerous to disturb a dog while he was eating. No doubt it was true, but damn it he wasn't about to wait for Jane to return.

He tried various approaches to getting free without ripping his clothes, including futile attempts at shaking off Pluto, bargaining with him and repeating the word *friend* until he felt like an idiot. Suddenly the shepherd jumped off barked loudly, then gently grabbed Max's hand with his mouth and led him down the hall to the kitchen. Toto scampered excitedly behind.

Pluto trotted over to a cabinet, opened it with his paw, then sat back on his haunches and barked three times.

"Well, I'll be a son of a gun," Max muttered as he retrieved several biscuits from the sack in the cabinet. Now he knew what "Max treat" was all about. It still didn't make up for his chewed jeans *or* his shredded dignity, but he had to admit that as far as Jane's safety went, if anyone was in danger it was probably Dr. Zodiac.

Crossing the hall, Max decided on his next move. First however, he'd best make sure the fire on the hearth was contained, although from his experience with her canine cops, Jane probably had them trained to stomp out fires too. With some reluctance, he had to face the possibility that Jane didn't really need a man in her life.

All that remained of the fire was a few smoldering logs, which to Max represented that brief scene of passion. Hunkering in front of the hearth, he let his fingers trail across the faded Oriental carpet, remembering the feel of Jane's body pressed against him, all warmth and softness.

He could have had her, he thought as a coil of desire rose within him. Then crushing down the thought, he stood. Max had never been a man to just take a woman, although there had certainly been enough who'd thrown themselves at him. Not Jane, though. What was it with the woman? Max wondered as he headed for the front door. She was attracted to him, and yet she persisted in perverse behavior.

"No more games," he informed the dogs, who bounded down the hall after him. Snatching up his coat, he hurried out the door before they got any ideas. Starting his car, he made a mental note to ask Jane whatever possessed her to train Pluto to do such clever tricks. That was just one of several questions he intended on asking her. The sixty-four-thousand-dollar question however, was one he had to ask himself: why on earth was he hung up on this maddening woman in the first place? And aside from boiling her in oil, just what was he going to do with her? Since every time he got near Jane, he either wanted to choke her or kiss her, he wondered if he'd ever find out.

Shoving these thoughts to one side, Max headed to the Astroscope storehouse. This time he was going to make sure nothing knocked him out.

The warehouse's exterior was exactly as he remembered. The interior however, on closer inspection, revealed a jumble of mannequins, costumes and an array of electronic gadgetry that told its own indicting story. Max, equipped with the flashlight and Polaroid camera that he always kept in his car, lost no time in carefully documenting everything. An examination of the catwalk revealed several sandbags tied precariously to the railing. Undoubtedly his clumsy entrance the other night had toppled one of them.

Impulsively, he decided to head to the paper and make some inroads into the mountain of unfinished work that awaited him. As for the photos, he was pretty sure Jane would be pleased to see them. Although he just might make her wait a bit for them.

Dr. Zodiac was going to be a little trickier to handle than Jane had first imagined, but she didn't want to think about that at the moment. After all, she'd managed to get out of the place without anything happening. It wasn't as if he'd chased her around the desk. But it was more the way he pressed her hand when he gave her Hannah's charts. Then of course, there was the glint in those beady little eyes. He looked at her as if he hadn't eaten in a long time and she were his next meal. His rambling on about other worlds and past lives made her even more antsy. As much as Jane hated to admit it, Max was probably right; she shouldn't have gone to see Dr. Z., and if Max hadn't acted so darn possessive, she might have listened to reason.

Reason. Ha! That had been Max's favorite word. Jane continued down St. Asaph's Street. The fact that she'd given Pluto that trick command was simply a last resort. Besides, by now Max was probably on his way home, cursing her. But that couldn't be helped. She'd apologize tomorrow morning, after she met with Hannah. Maybe she'd even take Max to lunch, sort of in celebration of his regaining his memory.

Stopping for a red light, she tried dismissing the events of the evening. But somehow the memory of his lips as they first met hers sent a tremor through her that was readable on the Richter scale, and despite everything, a warmth sprang up within her that cried out for his touch. She'd never known a simple kiss could practically take her to heaven but then, Max's kisses weren't all that simple. They were both tender and rough, demanding yet giving. Much like the man himself.

"Oh, Max," she said on a sigh, remembering the way his body fitted against hers, long and lean and yes, hard with undeniable desire. And she had responded with an abandon she'd never known, never imagined, shamelessly, greedily, as if at any moment he might be snatched away from her. Even now, her body ached with need, longed for his magic touch, yearned to take in what he had to offer.

A sharp honk from the car behind her jolted Jane back to the present as she accelerated and sped through the intersection. She swallowed hard against the feelings that Max had awakened in her. They were a lot deeper than she wanted to admit, they threatened her peace, tore away the curtain she'd so carefully drawn across her life. And they made her vulnerable.

Noticing her surroundings for the first time, she let out a groan. She'd done it again, ended up on a back street near the power plant. She was supposed to be going to *The Alexandrian,* not the moon. The fact that Pisces frequently wandered about in a fog was only one more irritating thing to deal with at this point.

Glancing in her rearview mirror, she noticed a dark Buick following her. Could it be the same one she'd seen outside of Astroscope? Abruptly she turned a corner, all too aware of her heartbeat and the slickness of her hands against the wheel. Great, she thought seeing the car some distance behind her.

Her sense of direction, never having been her long suit, totally abandoned her as she swung around another corner, only to find herself on a dark street by the river with the Buick practically on her tail. She swallowed hard, her mouth was as dry as cotton. As she threw on her high beams, her aging car came to a rattling halt, steam spewing from under the hood as a red light flashed on her dashboard.

Seeing her would-be assailant jump from his car was all it took to get Jane out of hers. With raw fear pounding in her skull, she ducked behind the front fender and as the man caught up with her, she darted out and with one swift jab of her foot, sent him to the ground. She heard him gasp, then call her name. Dear God, it was *Rufus!*

"Oh, no!" she cried, rushing to his side. "I'm so sorry! Oh Rufus, this is terrible."

"My fault," he said in a strained voice.

"You'd better catch your breath," Jane urged, kneeling down and putting a protective arm around him.

"Give me a minute... You know, you've got quite a kick. Learn that in karate class?"

"Madame Chian's Self-defense for Women," Jane explained hurriedly. "I get my certificate next month, but after this maybe I don't need it. Rufus, I'm really sorry."

"Don't worry about it."

"But I do. What if I'd killed you?"

"Don't let my compliment go to your head," he advised on a laugh. Then grimacing in pain, he said, "C'mon, I feel ridiculous sitting in the street."

"But what if something's broken?"

"Sitting here won't mend it," he said, taking her arm and getting to his feet. "What happened back there, anyway? Did old Blue Gem give up the ghost?"

"I think she needs a tune-up," Jane admitted as she guided Rufus to his car. "And you need the same. Are you in much pain?"

"Discomfort. You don't mind driving, do you?"

"Are you nuts? Of course not." Opening the passenger door she said, "We'll stop off at *The Alexandrian* and check you out. It's the closest point, unless you want to go to Potomac Emergency Room."

"Now you're the one who's nuts. You know how I feel about hospitals."

Sliding behind the wheel of his car, she said, "No, I didn't know. In an emergency though, they can save your life."

"Your kick wasn't that good, Jane. In fact—" he gingerly felt his ribs "—I think I'm okay."

"Thank God!" Jane expelled a sigh. "I'd have felt terrible if I'd broken anything."

"Not half as bad as I would have! By the way, what brought you down here anyway? A late-night swim?"

"It's a long story, Rufus," Jane said, turning the corner. "Which reminds me. Why were you following me? I mean, you *were* following me, weren't you?"

"I was wondering when you'd ask," Rufus replied somewhat sheepishly.

"We can exchange stories later," Jane suggested after a beat. "Take it easy for now."

"Do you think you're going to make a habit of this?" Rufus asked with a subdued laugh.

"A habit? Of what?"

"Rescuing wounded men."

"I've got a bottle of hydrogen peroxide in my desk," Jane said as they pulled into *The Alexandrian*'s parking lot.

"I'm really okay," Rufus protested, carefully unfastening his seat belt.

"It won't hurt to take a look," she countered as she clicked off the ignition. Then turning to Rufus, suddenly she said, "You know, if you'd been driving your Toyota instead of this monster I might have recognized you."

"It's my cousin's car. You see, I borrowed it so you wouldn't recognize me."

"Right," Jane said as she got out of the car. "And I'm sure it'll all make sense later." With a moan she stopped in her tracks and staring at Max's car said, "What is he doing here?"

"He's going to love this," Rufus muttered, following Jane to the back entrance. "Maybe now he'll believe you're a karate expert."

"I'm not an expert." Pausing at the door, she nervously chewed on her lower lip, then added to herself, "Well, it was done in good fun. It wasn't as if I meant to inflict damage."

"Good fun? No intention of inflicting damage?"

"Not exactly good fun," she corrected as she slowly opened the door. "Maybe if we're very quiet, Max won't know we're here."

"Hey, listen," Rufus said with a shrug, "if you don't want to tell him you attacked me in good fun, I won't."

Whirling around Jane exclaimed, "Oh Rufus, I wasn't referring to you! What I meant is...you see... Oh, dear, two in one night *does* look bad." Then pressing her index finger to her lips, she tiptoed down the hall to her office and quickly ushered in Rufus.

"I'm not suffering from amnesia, so you can tell me anything," he assured her, slowly sinking into a chair.

"That's part of the problem. Max regained his memory," she said in a hushed tone as she riffled through her desk drawer.

"That's great news."

"Except that he tried to stop me from going to Astroscope to pick up Hannah's chart, so I—I had Pluto detain him."

"What?"

"You see, Pluto and I have this game where he pretends to attack me, or anyone I tell him to— Now, Rufus, don't look at me like that.... Oh good, here's the peroxide. Why don't you take off your shirt—"

"And why don't you tell us both about the game?" Max drawled from his position by the door.

"Oh! you scared me." Jane cried as she jumped back.

"Consider it payback for having Pluto sit on me. He's not exactly a lapdog."

"I know that," Jane countered testily.

"So I was his treat for the evening," Max murmured as he slowly entered the room. "I'm surprised you and your crew haven't entered a circus. That dog is really well trained—squashed me to the floor and sat on me."

"Pluto *sat* on you?" Rufus asked, his head swiveling from Jane to Max.

"Oh, only for a few minutes. After I gave him his reward, I was free."

"You must have known all along he wouldn't hurt you," Jane said as she unobtrusively shoved the hydrogen peroxide back into the drawer. "Well, Rufus and I have some things to go over, so we'll see you later." She gestured hopefully toward the door, but Max didn't budge.

"I believe Rufus was about to disrobe? And from the looks of him, I'd say if must be a pretty good story. So, who's going to tell me about it?" Flexing his wrist, Max glanced at his watch. "Eleven o'clock ..."

"It was an accident!" Jane burst out as she snatched up the hydrogen peroxide again. "But you're so darn nosy, you just have to know everything!"

"If you found me in Camilla's office at this hour—or any hour, for that matter—and she was asking me to take off my shirt, even though I already looked like I'd been to the cleaners, wouldn't you be curious?" Max casually leaned one hip on the corner of Jane's desk and eyeing the bottle in her hand added, "Playing Florence Nightingale again?"

"It really was an accident," Rufus said as he lifted up his shirt. "Hey Jane, this doesn't look bad at all."

"But you can see where my heel hit your ribs. I'll just dab a little—"

"What did you say?" Max demanded, crossing over to them.

"I said you could see where my heel—you know, the heel of my shoe—hit his ribs." Turning away from Max, she gently applied some peroxide to Rufus's abrasion.

"I don't believe I'm hearing this," Max said, circling to face Jane.

"Well, believe it," she snapped, recapping the bottle and purposefully turning away. Then she asked Rufus, "Does it feel any better?"

"It's just a scratch."

"Tell me something," Max persisted, taking Jane by the shoulders. "Do you have something against men?"

"You're being ridiculous. It was an accident—"

"Your foot in his ribs? Were you practicing a new dance step?"

"She thought I was a mugger," Rufus interjected, patting his ribs.

"Rufus, *a mugger?*" Releasing Jane, Max passed his hand over his face, then ran it through his hair. "One of you want to tell me what's going on?"

"Rufus was following me down a dark street in a car I didn't recognize. My car sort of blew up, so I got out and ducked behind it—"

"Wait a minute, your car blew up?"

"Not literally. The point is, when Rufus caught up with me I let him have it." Dusting her hands as if dismissing the matter Jane turned to Rufus and said, "Anyway, you were about to tell me why you were following me."

"He was?" Max asked, stepping between them.

With a shrug, Rufus replied, "We'd better tell her."

"Oh brother, I have a feeling I'm going to love this one," Jane declared, sitting on her desk.

"I'm surprised you're not noting it down in your little black book," Max commented wryly.

"If it's that significant, I will. Go on Rufus, tell me why you felt compelled to follow me."

"It was for your own good," he began, looking from Jane to Max. "You see, we were afraid you might get into hot water. Well, that is, Max was. After tonight, you could probably walk down Fourteenth Street and take on all comers."

"Do you mean that Max hired you to tail me?"

"No, I did not hire him," Max snapped. "I simply felt that, given your impetuous tendencies, you needed a keeper." He sighed in an effort to forget about her incredible beauty. "Take a breath my dear, you're looking a little blue."

"I'll take a breath, all right. I only wish it were strong enough to blow you off this planet. But then I doubt any of the others would want you either. So, I've got impetuous tendencies, have I?'' She faced him squarely, amethyst fire leaping from her eyes. Idly he wondered what would happen if he kissed her right at that moment. He'd probably have more than a bruised rib for his trouble. Suddenly it struck him that he was actually enjoying their little contretemps.

"Well, aren't you going to say anything in your defense?'' she prompted.

I'm crazy about you, and if you'd give me half a chance, I'd tell you so you'd never forget. "My defense? I'm not the public menace,'' he replied with a shrug.

"You've got some nerve saying that! What if Rufus *had* been a mugger?'' She paced restlessly in front of him, darting dangerous looks in his direction.

"Then I'd have been right about your being in danger,'' he said with a raised eyebrow.

"Which justifies having Rufus as my keeper?''

"If you're going to slink around that part of town, you need one.''

"You're just irritated about Pluto—''

"The evening had promised other possibilities,'' Max reminded her, enjoying the spots of color that bloomed on her cheeks.

"I had to pick up those charts—''

"Yes, as I learned from your answering machine, you'll recall.''

"Hey, you two,'' Rufus called out, "I'm heading home. Be sure to lock up after I leave.'' As he started for the door however, Hannah burst in.

"Here you are!'' she said, then tried to catch her breath. "I couldn't imagine where you'd— What's this, a late-night conference?''

"That's one way to put it," Jane replied. "Would you mind following me in your car while I take Rufus home? You see—"

"Oh, I can drive, but I think I'll stick around until we've filled Hannah in on the latest," Rufus said, sitting back down. "And we'd also better call a tow truck for your car, Jane."

"All right, somebody begin!" Hannah said as she plopped onto the small couch. "What's the latest?"

Everyone looked at Jane, but it was the slightly amused expression on Max's face that made her heart do a curious flip-flop. It was almost as if he knew something about her that she didn't. How wrong she'd been to think that dismissing Max Hunter from her life would be easy.

Chapter Eight

By the time Jane updated Hannah, U Stall, We Haul Towing had phoned back saying they were running a little late, but would call again as soon as a tow truck was available.

"I'm surprised you didn't forecast all this with your stars," Max taunted.

"Everything?" Jane's eyebrows rose in mock surprise. "Right down to the fact that you'd put Rufus on my trail?"

"And a littered one, at that," he shot back, wondering why he was being so irritable with her. Earlier he'd been able to see the humor in it. Why not now?

With an inward sigh, he realized there were better things to dwell on, like the feel of her soft body pressed against him, like the way she returned his kisses and the undeniable hunger that sprang up between them.

"If you had trusted me," she said, "none of this would have happened."

"You're stealing my line. If *you* had trusted *me*—"

"Hey you guys," Hannah said, stepping into the fray, "we're all on the same side."

"Take a look at Rufus's ribs," Max suggested.

"They're fine," his friend protested.

"Indeed," Hannah said, nodding agreement. "Well Max, there's clearly no point in worrying about Janey! She can obviously take care of herself. It's the villains you should worry about! And if she doesn't get you with a karate kick, she can always clobber you in her column or her book."

"Book?" Max looked blankly from Hannah to Jane. "You're writing a *book?*"

"Heavens. It's not *that* unheard of."

"Oh. Some kind of romance?" Max asked, feeling a little left out of things and wondering why he hadn't been told.

"Sort of," Hannah replied.

"Not at all." Jane's mouth tightened, and as she looked away from him, Max noticed that her cheeks flamed with a rush of color.

"Janey's doing a book on astrological influences that make a man a good lover!" Hannah said on a triumphant note. "She's starting at the beginning with Aries and ending with Pisces."

"Sounds like you're working your way through the signs," Max commented, mildly wondering if he'd end up a footnote to Aries. Pushing this troublesome thought to one side, he cryptically added, "I wish you success in getting a publisher."

"No problem there," Hannah volunteered. "She's already got one."

"Oh?" Max felt his jaw tighten.

A sudden phone call from U Stall saying they were on their way cut off Jane's imminent response.

"I'll take you to your car," Max said as he got to his feet.

"Thanks, but I wouldn't dream of keeping you from all your work," Jane replied with a toss of red curls. "Rufus can drop me off."

"After his injuries?" Max asked as he moved toward her. He was still unsure of why she fascinated him. He certainly wasn't interested in being on the receiving end of one of her karate chops. But one thing he knew for sure was that he wanted her—and her dogs, swift kicks and fast talk weren't about to stop him now.

"Well . . . ?" he prodded. "Shall we?"

"Max has a point," Rufus interjected, giving his buddy a wink. "I think I'll just toddle on home."

"Me, too!" Hannah said. "But you're in good hands. See you tomorrow!"

"Hannah, wait. . . ." Whirling on Max, Jane let out a sigh. "You think you're really something, don't you?"

"Hey, not so fast," he said, throwing his hands up and taking a step back. "I'm not the one causing all the traffic jams."

"Mr. Innocence, I presume?" she grumbled over her shoulder, as she snatched up her purse. "Let's not keep U Stall waiting."

"My chariot awaits, m'lady," Max said with an exaggerated drawl as he followed her into the hallway.

"If you think you can just be my self-appointed keeper, then you'd better think again," she warned him.

"Thanks, but I've done enough thinking for one evening. This is simply a common courtesy." Stepping in front of her, he quickly reached the back door and pushing it open, smiled as she hurried past. "And I'm not going to gobble you up. . . yet."

If she heard this last comment, she cooly pretended not to, and after a few succinct directions as to where she'd left her car Jane fell silent.

Max knew they'd both run the gauntlet of emotions that evening. He also knew that if he took her in his arms, he just might not let her go this time. Perhaps the blow to his head had permanently dislodged his common sense. On the other hand, it might have knocked some into him. As for that astrology book she was writing, he preferred not to think about that, either. Surely her heated response to him wasn't just to fill the pages of some astro-how-to-land-a-man book. Or was it?

"See, I would have been perfectly safe waiting for the tow truck," Jane said as they arrived.

"They're late," Max observed, searching the dark street.

"You really didn't need to go out of your way."

"Maybe I wanted to," he countered softly. "Besides, this isn't the best area to hang out alone."

"You forget my karate kick."

"No, nor have I forgotten your dogs."

"Listen, about that—"

"It's over and done with," he said on a chuckle that surprised him. Then turning to her, he reached across the car seat and brushed back a lock of hair. "Tell me, why *did* you get a police dog?"

"Mom and Pops gave him to me. Pops is nuts about crime rates and he felt I needed protection."

"I could protect you." As his fingers began a slow massage along the nape of her neck, Max leaned toward her and brushed her lips with his, slowly claiming them. The feel of her mouth against his was guaranteed to drive him crazy. On a ragged breath, he pulled back. He'd gotten his memory back all right, every last bit of it. There was no way he'd be forgetting Jane Smith.

"Either we're about to be arrested or the tow truck has arrived," he said as a vehicle with flashing lights pulled up.

"It's the U Stall people," Jane confirmed, hastily disentangling herself from Max's arms. Whatever it was about Max she thought, he sure knew how to push the right buttons.

"I'll bet Blue Gem's one of their favorite customers," Max remarked as he got out of the car.

"Wait till yours is over ten years old," she shot back good-naturedly. As she headed for the tow truck, the heat of his gaze practically scorched her.

I should be exhausted, Jane thought as she padded barefoot from the bathroom to her bedroom, but I'm not. She paused before her dresser to inspect her face once again. It didn't look particularly kissed, although her cheeks were rosier than usual, and she had to admit her eyes had a certain glow.

"Enough!" she mumbled to her reflection. She had a lot to do tomorrow, and Max Hunter would have to go on the back burner. She'd be darned if he was going to give her a sleepless night.

She brushed her lips with the back of her hand, as if that might erase the memory of his kisses. But there was no getting around it, the man had kissed her as if he'd invented kissing.

Slipping into bed, Jane couldn't help conjuring up that last kiss. There she was trying to make a fast escape, but Max, who'd walked her to the door, had other things in mind. Before she could even get her key into the lock, he'd swept her into one of those toe-curling embraces. She'd wanted to say something clever or witty to him, but words wouldn't come. There was just his steady flow of kisses that encircled her face, worshipped her eyes and landed with an earth-shaking urgency on her lips.

"It's midnight," she'd finally managed to say between kisses.

"Pumpkin hour?" he'd asked, gently pinning her to the doorjamb. "Or do the hounds come out and drag you away?" His mouth descended once again, this time to that sensitive spot on her neck. Shivers went up her spine as he bit the tender skin. She felt herself shudder, heard his responding groan, then felt his large hands as they slid inside her coat and pulled her against him.

Sighing into her pillow, Jane turned onto her side, determined to keep Max out of her thoughts. At least until the Astroscope story was wrapped up. Exactly how she was going to do so remained to be seen, especially since Max insisted on having lunch with her after her astrological session with Hannah. Well, at least she'd managed to put off Dr. Zodiac until tomorrow night.

Dr. Zodiac. Given everything else that had happened, she probably should have told Max about her upcoming date with the man. Still, knowing how Aries men react to anything encroaching on their territory, perhaps it was best she hadn't mentioned it.

Wait a minute! Who said I was part of Max Hunter's territory?

Rolling onto her back, she let out a sigh of admission. Not only was she the guilty party, she'd slipped right into the role as if it had been custom-made for her.

She turned onto her other side again. She'd simply have to deal with that later. Lord knows she had enough on her plate, and probably not enough time to get everything done. Well, at least Blue Gem was going to pull through, or so the mechanic at the all-night service station assured her. The car would be ready for her tomorrow.

"So what do you think?" Hannah asked as she stacked the last jar of apple butter on the shelf.

"You want to do it *tonight?*" Jane said from her perch on a nearby stool.

"Sure." After jotting something down on her clipboard, she stuck the pencil behind her ear and beckoned for Jane to follow. "Give Dr. Z. another twenty minutes—just so he'll think we've been in consultation. Then call and tell him I've requested an immediate séance."

"I'm game if you are," Jane replied, following her friend down the narrow aisle of the Happy Harvest. Although it was a small and somewhat crowded grocery store, it was immaculate. Everything from its refrigerated produce section to the vast bins of nuts and grains was designed to make shopping an enjoyable experience.

"Super," Hannah remarked as they reached the glassed-in produce area. "I wonder if this is a good time to enlarge this section. I could move the seaweeds over there—" she gestured toward the herbs "—and then have room for more local produce. What do you think?" Opening the case, she pulled out a bright red strawberry and handed it to Jane. "They came in yesterday, best we've had in weeks."

Taking a bite of the juicy berry, Jane nodded in agreement, then after chewing thoughtfully for a moment,said, "Want me to pick an auspicious date for your renovations?"

"Would you?" Hannah grinned and tossed her another berry. "Consider that a down payment for services." Looking at her watch she murmured, "Oh boy, we open in ten minutes, and I'll bet Sherry's having the devil of a time at Tempeh Heaven. Oh well, come on in the office while I get the cash drawer ready."

"What's Sherry doing there?" Jane asked as she popped the berry into her mouth and followed her friend into an office the size of which prohibited all but the very slender from entering. The walls of the L-shaped room held floor-to-ceiling shelving that sagged under the weight of innumerable ledgers and books. A black door that sat on two sawhorses served as a desk, and the two wooden chairs that completed the furnishings were functional and reminiscent of grammar school.

"With everything going on, I guess I forgot to tell you that Sherry gave notice at The Golden Garter, and while she's deciding if she wants to go back to Boston, she's pinch-hitting for me and is picking up our Wednesday shipment of tempeh. They make great stuff over there, but I think they're still a little spaced out from the sixties."

"Sherry at Tempeh Heaven?" Jane's eyebrows rose. "No, that wasn't what I originally had on my mind. But I'll bet Rufus will be happy to hear about this."

"Oh, guess I didn't tell you that either. After all that hoopla last night, he stopped by The Golden Garter, had a drink and asked her to dinner. Mind you, this is a man with broken ribs—"

"Bruised," Jane corrected somewhat guiltily.

"Well, whatever they are they didn't stop him from making all the right moves. What sign is he anyway?"

"Aries, the week after Max."

"But they're so different," Hannah pointed out as she reached into the safe and pulled out the cash box. "Go on, I can listen and count."

"Rufus has nice tidy Virgo keeping him in check, whereas Max..."

"Yes?" Hannah slanted a knowing glance in Jane's direction. "What exactly is Max? Interested in you, I hope."

"I don't know why you don't go into the matchmaking business and be done with beans and apple butter."

"I'm only a part-time Cupid. It's sort of like a hobby." Hannah unceremoniously dumped quarters into the cash drawer. "You know, he *will* forgive you for siccing Pluto on him. I bet years from now, he'll consider it one of the high points of your relationship."

"Right. But for now, let's get back to business."

"Séance on a Stormy Evening," Hannah whispered, cracking open a roll of dimes as if she were making an omelette. "I wonder if Dr. Z. will be able to conjure up the spirit of Cousin Melrose." With a chuckle she said, "He's hale and hearty in Palm Beach, and would love the idea of being passed off as my dearly departed and filthy-rich husband."

"Be prepared to see him, then."

"You really think so?"

"I'll just about bet the ranch on it. You see, I stopped by the library on the way over here and did a little research on holograms. Evidently it really is possible to project an image into space from a photograph or as in Sherry's case, from actual film footage."

"Okay Janey, call our man at Astroscope and see if we can't get the ball rolling for this evening." Picking up the cash drawer, she headed for the office door. "Time to let in the hungry masses." She paused then asked, "I guess you don't want Max to know about our new adventure yet, do you?" Without waiting for a reply, she left.

Max. Even the sound of his name gave Jane a heady rush as warring emotions jockeyed for top billing. Why did it have to be so complicated? She should tell him about the séance, but he'd probably go through the proverbial Aries roof. Reaching for the phone, Jane told herself she didn't have to tell him every little thing she did. After all, she didn't clear her daily column with him, and he probably didn't even know she wrote the weekly "Just Ask Greta." So why did she feel she had to tell him about something as innocent as a séance?

Cradling the phone against her shoulder, she thumbed through her address book for Astroscope's number, and finding it, punched it in.

The séance was a great way to get firsthand information for her story. She just hoped it didn't look too rushed to Dr. Zodiac. Jane had originally thought it should be done the next week, but Hannah was probably right. Strike while the iron was hot. The question was, would Dr. Z. believe Hannah's immediate need for communicating with dear departed Melrose?

"Dr. Zodiac?" Jane said. "I have great news for you...."

Ten minutes later, after listening to his monologue on enchained souls, and how—with scientific aids—he had been able to tap into the great reservoir of the hereafter, which Jane translated as meaning rich clients' wallets, he agreed to the impromptu séance.

"Do you think you can handle a seven-thirty encounter in the Upper Chamber?" Jane asked Hannah as she plunked a dollar on the counter for a carob-covered rice bar.

"Upper, middle or lower, this is one trip I don't want to miss. Imagine, Cousin Melrose in 3-D!" Pushing the dollar toward Jane she added, "My treat. Oh, by the way, Sherry's unloading tempeh in the walk-in and she wants to come with us. But I said she'd have to check with you."

"Sure, it'll be like old-home week," Jane replied on a laugh then peeling back the cellophane, she sunk her teeth into the crunchy delight of her rice bar.

Sherry was in the midst of unsuccessfully heaving a carton of tempeh onto a shelf in the refrigerated walk-in when Jane made a timely appearance. Stepping forward, she caught a corner of the carton and helped Sherry slide it into place.

"That was the last one," Sherry said, brushing the back of her arm across her forehead as she sank onto a stool outside the walk-in.

"Are you sure you want to quit The Golden Garter so soon?" Jane teased, sitting across from her on a step stool. Then breaking off a piece of carob delight, she passed it to Sherry.

"Thanks. Boy, is this going to hit the spot." Waving the snack in midair Sherry added, "I'm just doing this to fill up time and help out Hannah. I guess she told you about Rufus showing up after my show last night." She grinned, then stuck the snack in her mouth.

"He has remarkable resilience," Jane said, "especially considering what he went through, so I would take it as a definite green light." Jane watched as Sherry chewed and nodded. Even though she was dressed in faded jeans and a baggy white shirt, she looked radiant. Her white-blond hair was pulled back in a long braid, and her face, devoid of all makeup, had a light sheen of perspiration on it.

"That was quite an evening you all had last night. If only he'd told me he was... Well, your body guard, I wouldn't have felt so funny about our broken date." Rubbing her hands along the sides of her jeans, Sherry let out a sigh. "But he's taking me to Manakin Farms for lunch this afternoon, so that should make up for last night. By the way, do you think it will be all right if I tag along for this séance tonight?"

"Sure. In fact, since you're down as having referred Hannah, your being there would make perfect sense. Oh, but don't tell Rufus about it. You see, I'm sort of keeping this to myself."

"And from Max, right?" Sherry jumped to her feet and briskly dusted her hands against her jeans. "Well, got to check in with Hannah but don't worry, my lips are sealed."

By lunchtime, Jane had managed to whip through her daily column and make significant inroads on the weekly "Just Ask Greta" column. Most of her letters were fairly typical: love, money, career and health. Understandably enough, the love queries usually outnumbered the others. The irony of advising others on this area of their lives didn't escape Jane. Then of course, there was the old saying that "we teach what we need most to learn." That aphorism neatly applied to this week's petitioner who, feeling haunted by her cruel ex-husband, wanted to know when, if ever, she would be able to accept the love of her current boyfriend. Jane was in the midst of studying three very complex charts when Max appeared in her doorway.

"I stopped by earlier, but I take it you slept in." He was leaning against the doorjamb as if he were holding the thing up, and Jane further noticed an amused look in his eye.

"I did not sleep in—"

"I wouldn't blame you if you had. That was quite an evening you had last night." Pushing away from the wall, he slowly crossed the room, then stopped at the edge of her desk. His grin practically took up his entire face. "We have a lunch date, remember?" He reached over and snatched up one of her books.

"I hadn't forgotten," Jane said, attempting to force her attention back to the charts. With a sigh, she slapped her pencil onto the desk and tapping her watch said, "We agreed on one-thirty. That gives me another half hour to work."

"Oh, don't let me stop you—"

"You're the editor-in-chief, for Pete's sake. Don't you have anything better to do than catch up on your reading in my office?" She swallowed hard, knowing that her face had just gone red. "You can borrow it, if you like," she muttered, returning to her astrological data.

"But it's a present for your…niece, I believe. Or was that the other one, something about Larkspurs. This one's *The Whispering Statue*." He wagged the book in front of her nose.

"Look, call me a crank and leave it at that." She shot him a killing look from beneath her lashes. "You'll probably never understand, but I collect old books. I have an entire attic filled with them. And as you've probably guessed, they're all fairy tales—Oz books, Nancy Drew, Yellow, Blue and Red Fairy Tale Books." Gesturing toward the book in Max's hands she added, "I picked that one up this morning at an antique store on my way down King Street. As habits go, it beats gambling. Now if you'll let me get back to my column,

I'd appreciate it." If she got any hotter or her cheeks any redder, she'd probably explode.

Max slipped the book back onto Jane's desk and said, "Who knows what would have happened to me if you hadn't played detective the other night. Perhaps I have Nancy Drew to thank, after all." He headed for the door, only to pause there and say, "I'm referring to the storeroom incident."

She knew darn well what he meant. Picking up her pencil, she returned to what she seemed to do best.

"I wasn't making fun of you," he said softly in her ear as he pulled out her chair for her at the Wharf Restaurant. He noticed that she was wearing that scent again whatever it was and it made him crazy. "I really wasn't," he asserted as he took the chair opposite her. The table between them was covered with white linen, silver place settings and a bouquet of daisies.

"I never said you were," Jane replied, blinking her lovely eyes back at him. "Though if you were there was probably just cause," she added with a rueful grin. Retrieving her napkin, she leaned back while the waiter filled their water glasses.

"You're certainly different from most women," Max said, hoping that it didn't sound as though he was delivering a line. "And I like that." He watched as spots of faint color appeared once again on her cheeks, and he ached to reach across the table and touch her slender white hand.

"Wine would probably put you to sleep, wouldn't it?" he asked, at a clear loss to say anything else.

"I think ice tea would be better," she replied with a sweetness that totally disarmed him. "And a Chef's salad minus the ham, chicken and cheese—"

"Why don't you just get a tossed salad?" he asked
reasonably.

"No. I like the lettuce they use in the Chef's salad, and
I want them to put in anchovies and black olives." Her
smile suddenly bloomed and leaning across the table she
added, "Haven't you noticed that the world's divided
into two camps. Those who love anchovies and those
who hate them?"

"How very political of you to notice." Max eyed her
mischievous expression and grinned. Then catching the
waiter's eye, Max gave their order.

Toward the end of lunch, Jane couldn't keep it to
herself any longer and putting her fork down with a
clatter, she dug into her purse and pulled out the envelope whose contents had sent her into giggles that
morning. "Take a look at these!" she exclaimed,
thrusting the envelope across the table. Leaning back in
her chair, she watched as Max slowly sifted through one
photograph after another.

"Those are from my return call to Astroscope's
storeroom," she gurgled, then seeing the sharp look he
sent her, she quickly added, "Oh now Max, I had to at
least try to get some photographs. It would have helped,
of course, if I had taken the lens cap off first."

"I should be angry with you," Max said passing the
photos back to her, then with a mysterious look she
couldn't fathom, he took an envelope out of his breast
pocket and slowly nudged it across the table. "However, as you'll see, that base is covered now. But I
wouldn't mind going back and doing a bit more investigating. That is, if you're game."

"What do you mean, 'that base'?" Jane paused, then
looking from the photograph in her hand to Max's
grinning face she added, "You sneak!"

"Ah. Pot calling the kettle black. Tsk, tsk. And here I thought you'd be pleased."

With a laugh she said, "I am, you crazy man! Though I'm also curious as to how long you'd planned on holding out on me."

"Me holding out on you? That's a good one. At any rate, I thought you might like to have these for your story."

Looking up from the photos, Jane flashed him a smile. "Thanks. I really do appreciate it." Slipping the photos into their envelope, she started to pass them back to Max.

"Keep them. I thought I might go back tonight. Want to come with me?"

"Tonight?" Picking up her fork, she pierced the last anchovy.

"Why not?"

"Well, you see... I've got plans." Jane watched as Max's face fell about two inches.

"Oh. Plans. Well... then we could do it tomorrow, I suppose."

Jane puckered her lips, as if the anchovy had suddenly gone bad. "How about Friday night?" she asked in a bright and very false voice.

"I thought you were so keen on getting this astrology-scam story put to bed—"

"I am, I am," she quickly reassured him as she took refuge in the dessert menu.

"Okay, Miss Drew. What gives?"

"I thought I'd have a peach cobb—"

"You're up to something again. What is it this time?" Snatching the menu from her, Max captured her hands in his. "Haven't you got it through your exceedingly pretty head that I care what happens to you?"

"It's not that big a deal. But you'll probably think so," she said. Reluctantly, she met his gaze. "Tonight Hannah, Sherry and I are going to Astroscope for a séance. But before you start issuing orders, rest assured I'll be well protected."

With a sigh, Max patted her hand. "You weren't going to tell me about it, were you?"

"Actually, I *was* thinking about telling you." Her gaze dropped to his hands; they were still resting lightly on hers. It was a caring, gentle gesture, one that brought an unexpected lump to her throat. She didn't want this, didn't need this.

She looked up at him and saw the tenderness in his eyes, and beneath it, an eagerness held at bay. Suddenly another layer of her carefully constructed defenses melted.

She cared for him. Oh, how she cared, she realized as her eyes lingered on his face for a moment longer. Max Hunter wasn't one of her illusive fairy-tale lovers, nor was he the blond charmer she had thought him to be. He was just Max: the kind of man she'd always wanted and so secretly feared finding.

Chapter Nine

"Well I for one, am glad you told Max," Hannah said as they pulled into Astroscope's parking lot, "because it doesn't do to hold back in a relationship. And for heaven's sake, don't tell me you all aren't interested in each other."

"Maybe just a little," Jane allowed cautiously as she clicked off the ignition. "Still, he didn't have to refer to the three of us as Nancy, Bess and George."

"*Who?*" Sherry asked from the back seat.

"Nancy Drew and her side kicks," Hannah answered on a laugh as she stepped out of the car.

"He *could* have compared us to the Three Stooges," Sherry put in.

"Don't even suggest it," Jane murmured, looking up at the impressive Victorian brick that housed Astroscope. "Well ladies, shall we?"

They were greeted at the door by the receptionist, who if possible, looked even more like the Wicked Queen than before. Her pallor contrasted sharply with the blood-red lipstick that suggested a Draculean feast. Dr. Z.'s secretary in black velvet, swished behind her and together they led a silent candlelight procession to the Upper Chamber.

"Is this for real?" Hannah whispered after the honor guard had left the three women in a vaulted room.

"Shh, not so loud," Jane admonished as she crossed to what had to be the séance table. It was small, round and covered with a lace cloth. In the center was a bowl of water and two flickering purple candles.

Idly, Hannah ran her fingers across the rim of the covered table. "Right, Cousin Melrose might hear me. Oh Mel, I do wish you were here. You'd love it!" Then turning to Sherry she asked, "Does this thing lift off?"

"No, but it shakes a little, then a puff of smoke comes out from over there." She indicated a velvet-lined niche that was illuminated by several purple spotlights. "And what I thought was my husband's ghost appeared right about where I'm standing."

"The hologram no doubt," Jane said, eyeing the beams overhead. "Well, we've got ringside seats."

"If it's like before, it'll be quite a performance," Sherry said with a shiver. "Although I was so keyed up and—" She whirled around just as Dr. Zodiac, flanked by his assistants, entered through a sliding door on the far side of the room. He paused on seeing Sherry, then with a nod of recognition, floated forward.

"Why, Mrs. Devereaux, this is a pleasure indeed. Ah, but you're the one who referred Mrs. Ritchie, aren't you?"

"Yes. I got so much out of my communication with Tommy that I felt certain you could help my friend."

Taking the initiative, Hannah held out her hand and introduced herself in what Jane considered an Academy Award performance. There was the appropriate tremble in her voice, and as Hannah sat in the indicated chair, she seemed as if she might burst into tears at any moment.

Lord, don't overdo it, Jane thought, quickly sitting beside her and nudging Hannah's knee.

It was all Jane could do to keep a straight face when Dr. Zodiac fanned out his arms like a bat and intoned, "Let us begin our journey." She'd seen something similar to this on the late-night horror show.

Dr. Z.'s two assistants melted into twin puddles on either side of him. Then after a moment's silence, they laid their long, pale hands on the lace-covered table and began to hum.

"Ladies, we shall now prepare to invoke the spirit of Melrose Ritchie," Dr. Z. boomed out as he settled into an intricately carved, highbacked chair.

Melrose Ritchie? Jane bit down on her lower lip, sucked in her cheeks and managed to keep a straight face. Risking a glance to her right, she saw that Hannah was staring raptly at their mentor. Sherry was also playing an admirable part. As for the two raven-headed Gorgons, it was better not even to look at them, Jane resolved. Her microcassette was recording the session, but for the moment, there wasn't a lot she could do except watch and wait.

The waiting didn't take long. Almost immediately the table began to tremble ever so slightly. And even though she knew it was a trick, it *was* unnerving. The chandelier above them dimmed considerably, but Jane's eyes were glued to the candles before them. They were flickering wildly, but miraculously stayed flush with the table. The bowl of water sloshed gently, and the lights dimmed even more.

"Is anyone there?" Dr. Z. asked from his trancelike pose. His eyes were closed, and he sat as erect as a gravestone. "One knock, yes, two knocks, no."

Jane waited for the puff of smoke.

"Spirit, you have nothing to fear. You are among loved ones. One knock for yes..." At the sound of a distinct knock, the table rocked some more, the lights blacked out, the expected smoke billowed into the room and the assistants screamed and fell forward across the table.

"I sense a presence," Dr. Z. murmured, rising from his chair, "over there!" He pointed suddenly toward a faint glow that melted through the smoke.

"It's...it's...*Melrose!*" Hannah let out a gasp and half rose from her chair. "Melrose speak to me. Tell me what to do."

"It's just like with Tommy," Sherry murmured. "Miraculous."

It sure is, Jane thought as she watched the flickering image before them. What a con game.

"He wants to know if you have a specific question for him?" Dr. Zodiac asked after a moment.

"Oh yes," Hannah murmured. "I just don't know where to begin."

"Perhaps just one question for this initial visit. Whatever is most plaguing you. But remember, once the vision fades, I'll be unable to intercept the messages for you. We must also be careful not to tax his strength too much. You see, it's always hard the first time out for them."

I'll bet it is, Jane decided, fingering the minicamera that was tucked in her skirt pocket. What a show! Dr.

Z., looking like a generic vampire, flanked by the wicked queens and in the distant mist their very own ghost, courtesy of Cousin Melrose.

"Well," Hannah began, "most of all I want to send him my love."

Dr. Zodiac paused, then swaying slightly he slowly intoned, "He senses that, and he's happy you've contacted him."

"But I suppose what's really on my mind is our estate. If only Mel could tell me what to do with the money," Hannah said with an appropriately dramatic note. Jane was quite sure Dr. Z. could interpret that query with the greatest of ease.

"You hear her, do you not spirit? One knock for yes, two for no." A distinct knock shattered the ensuing silence.

"What should I do?" Hannah repeated.

"We must give the spirit time to consider an answer," Dr. Z. said.

"But what if he fades away?"

"Very well. We can try." He paused, then after a moment asked, "Should Mrs. Ritchie reflect on how to handle her finances? One knock for yes, two knocks for no." There was a short pause followed by a soft knock.

"More reflection?" Hannah choked out the question as she dabbed at her eyes.

"I think we'll not get an immediate answer, as I sense he is fading to the other side. May I add Mrs. Ritchie, that you mustn't be too hasty," Dr. Z. warned. "The world is full of unscrupulous people, those weighed down with greed. This is a serious matter that will require the most delicate handling. I am of course at your service."

"Oh, I'm so grateful." Twisting her hanky, Hannah added, "Perhaps you're the one to give me financial direction."

At Dr. Z.'s modest nod, Jane wanted to stand up and cheer. The man couldn't have been more obliging if he'd tried.

"Wait. There is more. Your loved one wishes you to know he is pleased you've contacted him, but due to the strain of crossing over, he must leave. But he begs you to come again for further consultation."

Bingo! Jane thought. Dr. Z.'s eyes were still closed, but he was slowly coming out of his trance, so it was now or never. Aiming the minicamera at Cousin Melrose's specter, she snapped a quick shot. Whether it would stand up in court was inconsequential; it would suit her story. Slipping the camera back into her pocket, she watched as the "ghost" faded from view.

As the lights slowly came on, the assistants rallied themselves and with a zombielike demeanor, glided from the room. Dr. Zodiac waited a moment after opening his eyes then said, "This was a particularly powerful encounter, even though it was a short one. Sometimes we get no contact at all."

I'll bet, Jane thought, patting the pocket that held her camera.

"I only hope it has not been too stressful for you, Mrs. Ritchie," Dr. Zodiac intoned.

"Oh no, Dr. Zodiac, it was an illumination," Hannah answered brightly. "I feel so at peace. And of course, I'll have to come again." Rising to her feet, she added, "I'll just settle up with your assistants and make an appointment for next week."

"Splendid!" he replied. His eyes reminded Jane of the comic-book characters who blinked dollar signs.

"I've got to hand it to you all," Jane said as they pulled out of the parking lot some ten minutes later, "you really had that old imposter eating out of your hands."

"Back in summer camp, Sherry and I were in charge of skits. Guess we still work well as a team."

"So that's your secret!"

With a laugh, Hannah snapped her seat belt in place. "Yep. You know, tonight was kind of fun. Although I have to say when that table started tilting, so did my insides. It must have scared you half to death that first time it happened, Sherry."

"Almost," the blonde agreed. "But not tonight. And I'll be real happy to see him get what's coming to him." With a smile she settled back in her seat. "Thanks to you all, it won't be long."

"Not if I can help it," Jane vowed as she stopped for a red light. "Who knows, I might even wrap things up tomorrow night."

"Janey, are you sure you want to keep that little date with him?" Hannah asked.

"You won't have us with you," Sherry reminded her.

"If I did, it might be a little too cozy," Jane countered, "but I appreciate your concern."

"Hey kiddo, we do care about you."

"Hannah, you're beginning to sound like Max."

"Good for Max! You know, there's something solid about that man."

"Looks can be deceiving."

"He *is* good looking," Sherry slipped in on a sigh.

"Oh, I'm talking about something much more substantial than cleft chins, blue eyes and rippling muscles," Hannah joked. "I'm talking character. He's not

hung up on his ego. He'll always be there for you...
and—oh Lord, Janey, can't you see that the man's
madly in love with you? Maybe you're the one who
needs to get conked on the head. Better yet, come on by
and have Nicky stick a few well-placed needles in you."

"Just what I've always wanted!" Jane said. "By the
way, when does he get back?"

"Next week, and you're avoiding the topic."

"Topic?"

"Yes. Max, remember?"

"My memory's fine, and—"

"And from what you've told me, so is his. His memory's fine, his personality is dream material, his body has
Helen Gurley Brown's stamp of approval—"

"In other words, she'd definitely invite him into her
parlor," Jane said with a laugh.

"For starters," Hannah replied. "But your home-
work, oh Janey, my dear friend, is to let go and just let
it happen. Because something tells me that Max Hunter
will do the rest."

Jane's cheeks felt as though hot coals had been
pressed into them. Everything Hannah said was right on
target. But Jane was still scared. What would happen
five years down the road? She knew it was crazy, but
despite all the articles she'd read to the contrary, a committed relationship still meant giving up control, and
Jane wasn't sure she could afford to do that.

After she dropped Hannah and Sherry off, Jane drove
across the Fourteenth Street Bridge into Washington,
D.C., and looped around the Tidal Basin. It was a mild
night, so she rolled down the windows, opened the sun-
roof and allowed her thoughts to tumble about her as she
breathed in the lush night air. In another few weeks, the
cherry blossoms in all their frothy finery would line the

circular path around the Jefferson Memorial. What a glorious sight that always was.

Pulling into a parking area by the memorial, she got out of the car and headed down a grassy bank to the edge of the Tidal Basin. A playful breeze rippled off the water, carrying the fresh scent of spring rain. Like an impatient lover, it nipped at Jane's face and lifted her hair in a soft caress. Max's caress.

She sat on an iron bench positioned at the water's edge, and stared at the pale golden dome of the Jefferson Memorial. Its reflection, which shimmered softly in the Tidal Basin, reminded Jane of an impressionist painting.

"Max cares about me," Jane murmured, resting back against the cool wrought-iron. So why was she frightened of having a relationship?

"But I haven't known him long enough," she protested, propping her elbows on her knees and leaning forward. Maybe the attraction was simply chemistry? All that supposed love and passion reduced to a couple of hormones. Not exactly a heartening thought.

On the drive home, Jane resolved to let down her defenses, at least enough so she could get her bearings on the relationship. Her thoughts, however, took a nosedive as she pulled in behind Max's parked car.

Collecting herself and taking a deep breath, Jane got out of the car and was debating whether or not to go tap on his car window when he slowly unfolded his lanky frame, stepped out of his car and turned to face her. Even at fifteen feet, she could make out the glint in his eye—or maybe it was the set of his shoulders or his deliberate stance.

She hesitated, then moved forward. "Hi!" She willed a cheerful nonchalance into her voice.

"Do you know what time it is?"

"Do we have a—a date or something?" Lord, she hated it when she did her pussyfoot Piscean routine.

"No, tonight was Dr. Zodiac, remember?"

"Of course. And I guess you've come for the low-down, right?"

"Sort of, although Sherry filled me in pretty much. And I thought—"

"Sherry?"

"Rufus brought her by before they went out. That's why I figured you'd be back. And so I waited." He leaned a hip against his car and slowly crossed his arms in front of him. "And waited."

"I *am* sorry. But after I dropped Hannah and Sherry off, I sort of felt like a drive, so I..." Jane paused, knowing only too well what Max would think of her nocturnal touring.

"So you what?"

"Oh, went to—to look at the cherry blossoms," she replied, moving quickly toward the sidewalk.

"The trees aren't in bloom yet," he said smoothly, countering her move and blocking the path.

"Another couple of weeks and they'll be out. Anyway, it was a nice drive, and I'm sorry I kept you waiting. But then, since I didn't know you were here—"

"You probably got out and took a midnight stroll around the memorials, didn't you?"

"It's not midnight.... Well, it wasn't then. And I didn't take a stroll. I sat on a bench by the Jefferson Memorial—"

Closing the gap between them, he pulled her into his arms. "What am I going to do with you?"

"I haven't the slightest idea. But if you don't kiss me..."

He did.

"That's for starters," he said in a husky voice when the kiss finally ended. "And I've got a lot of things in between," he whispered in her ear. Then nibbling on her neck he added, "And I've got a finale that will knock your socks off."

"I get the picture," Jane replied breathlessly as a liquid heat rolled over her. Then with her hands pressed against his chest, she stepped back. "My neighbors think that I'm a—"

"*Nice* girl?" At her affirmative nod he tacked on, "And you are, Greta-Jane. Believe me, you are. I wouldn't worry about the neighbors though, since it's after midnight."

"Mr. Slavinski—he's the neighbor on my left—he knows everything that everyone does. And the lady who lives next door to him is . . ."

Max's lips were on hers once again, muffling her nervous protests.

"We could go inside, you know," he whispered against her parted lips. "Wouldn't want to upset Mr. Slavinski. Though you'll have to promise not to sic Pluto on me." He drove his fingers through her silky hair, and pulling her against him once again, wondered how much longer he could hold out. He'd sat in his car for almost an hour before circling Astroscope's headquarters. He'd even checked out the storehouse by the railroad tracks, and then he'd come back to her town house to wait for her. A half hour of that and he was practically going nuts. Then when she finally showed up, she told him she was sitting by the Jefferson Memorial!

Max was not a patient man, and feeling her soft curves press against him didn't help matters any. He dropped his hands to her shoulders, then slipping them beneath her lightweight cape, he sought out the swell of her hips, and dragging her even closer, he growled out her name and reveled in her whimpered response. He'd wanted to chew her out, tell her what a fool she'd been to involve herself in this damn astrology caper, but the taste of her drove those thoughts to the nether regions of his brain.

On a sigh, he drew back and looked into her dew-filled eyes, felt her longing as it streaked through him like a shaft of summer lightning, then felt the tug on his hand as she turned and led him up the brick walk to her door.

As soon as they entered the hallway, they slipped out of their coats and fell into an embrace. His hands moved down the length of her slender back, then circled her waist and moved lower. All the while he kissed her eyes, forehead, then nipped at her earlobes. There was a heady, sweet fragrance about her that made him want to devour her, inch by throbbing inch. He felt her fingernails dig into the fabric of his shirt and heard her responding moan as his palms skimmed across her taut breasts. Lowering his head, his mouth followed this path as his fingers opened pearl buttons on a silk top.

''Oh, Janey,'' he murmured as his tongue smoothed across her full breasts. Eagerness fired his need to stroke and fondle her, to take her to him as he had with no other woman. He heard and felt her breath come in a rush. It was all there: the need, the passion, the urgency.... And yet neither of them had voiced their feelings. He had pursued and she had run. Until now.

Max had waited until her vulnerability was at its pitch, and then he'd moved in. That wasn't his style. He was ardent and determined, but aboveboard. Pulling back, he managed to fasten the two top buttons of her blouse. His hands were shaking, his heart was racing and his mouth was about as dry as a desert.

"Janey... I know this is going to sound strange, but this isn't exactly what I came over for. What I mean is..." He reached for her hands and held them; they were cool, loving hands.

"It's okay," she said in a low voice. "We—we seem to have this effect on each other."

"It's more than that, Janey, and you know it. I want you to know though, that I'm sorry if I seemed to be rushing you." He squeezed her hands and added, "Hey, you can look at me. I don't bite heads off."

"I never said you did."

"But you've thought it."

"Occasionally," she allowed in a shaky voice. Then withdrawing her hands from his, she bent down and scooped up their wraps and hung them on pegs. "How about a cup of tea?"

"No. No more food or drink until after we've talked." Taking her hand, he added, "By the way, where are the canine cops?"

"In the dog run out back," she replied breathlessly. "Listen Max, I don't know whether I'm coming or going when I get around you, and—"

"I'm going to try to straighten that out," he said, leading her into the living room. "Why don't we sit down for a few minutes? Talk, just talk," he promised as he pulled her onto the velvet couch.

Jane looked at him carefully then said, "You accuse me of driving *you* nuts? Do you have any idea what your current style is doing to me?"

"Randolph Smith's daughter can handle anything," Max said on a chuckle that surprised him. "After all, the Smiths are sturdy stock. Wasn't his motto, 'Get the truth, but don't forget the scoop'?"

"Something like that," Jane replied, reclaiming her hand. "But that doesn't have a lot to do with me."

"Oh, I think it does," he said, dropping his hand onto her shoulder. "It's what attracts you to me. Your spunk. Well, that and a few other things." Slowly he began caressing her neck.

"It's late, Max. Why don't we talk about this tomorrow." There was a quaver in her voice, and he sensed she was about to put up her armor. Maybe talking wasn't such a good idea, after all he reflected.

"I've got meetings all morning and some new printing equipment coming in the afternoon. And then, unless you forget, you've got some mysterious date in the evening." Turning toward her, he added, "Am I right?"

"There's always the next day," she said, turning her eyes from his gaze.

"You never did tell me what it is you're doing tomorrow night." He stroked the back of her neck, then noticing the slight blush in her cheeks, knew she was keeping something from him again.

"Well?" he prompted at last.

"It's—it's nothing, really."

"Then cancel it."

"Look, once this Astroscope story is in the bag, I'll spend an evening interviewing you for this book I'm doing. That should make your Aries ego happy." Abruptly she stood up, stretched and let out a yawn.

She smiled at him. He didn't return the sentiment. Could it be that he knew about her date with Dr. Zodiac? Impossible!

Well, maybe not so impossible. After all, he hadn't even bothered to ask much about the séance.

"So, is it a date?" she asked with forced gaiety.

"Sure, put me in your book. I forgot that you're researching the perfect lover. And since Aries is at the beginning, I guess you want to get on with it." Slowly he stood, crossed toward her, then after a moment merely said, "Good night, Jane."

She watched as his large frame disappeared out her front door, then listened as his boot heels clicked resolutely on the brick walk. She didn't move a muscle, but strained to listen for the sound of his car as it started then pulled away. The clock struck one, and with a sigh Jane headed for the back door. She'd let the dogs in and try not to think about how lonely she felt.

"You're a fool, Jane Smith," she muttered to herself. But after her "date" with Dr. Zodiac, things would be different. Maybe then she'd feel safe enough to let Max into her heart. Maybe then she'd be able to trust her feelings again. After all, she was a Pisces, and hadn't they written the book on feelings? Weren't they the ones with the arrow-straight intuition?

Max lay awake, watching the shadows on the ceiling and thinking. Life had always been fairly easy for him. He simply gathered his facts and acted. It had always been a matter of who, what, why, when and where. Then Janey had come along. She asked questions he'd never even thought of. It didn't seem to bother her that there might not be answers. Max went for the goal, and she went for the ride.

He knew without a doubt he had to have Jane, and this time nothing was going to stop him. She was the goal, the ride, the whole meaning of his life. How on earth had he done without her? And what would he do if she wouldn't have him?

Once again he wondered what the devil she was up to tomorrow night. She'd neatly avoided telling him, and that usually meant trouble. He'd see about that.

Trouble was something Max knew how to handle. With a little luck, he'd also find out how to handle Janey Smith.

Chapter Ten

Max had made just about every excuse in the book to visit Jane's office that morning, until she pointedly reminded him that he had appointments. His memory was doing fine he assured her, although he was in fact getting an aerobic workout by dashing down the hall to see Jane between those tightly scheduled appointments.

She was up to something and he intended to find out exactly what. On his third visit, under the pretext of filling up his coffee cup, she practically jumped out of her chair. She was as skittish as a mouse. But there was nothing mousey about the pink silk dress she was wearing. It had a scooped neck and a waterfall of soft lace down the front. Not your basic office outfit, although he had to admit that on Jane it looked sensational. The skirt skimmed the tops of her knees, and the view of her lovely long legs sent the blood drumming through Max's veins. Being around her made him feel as though spring had really arrived.

Still, he reminded himself, she was keeping something from him. Hoping to make inroads over a leisurely lunch, he tried luring her to Neptune's Table but with no success.

"I've got to get this column done," she murmured, barely looking up at him.

"Thought you always finished that before lunch," he remarked off-handedly, moving into the room.

"My *other* column," she replied as her fingers flew across the computer keyboard. Pausing, she glanced in his direction, "'Just Ask Greta.'"

"Oh, right." Damn, she had fingers in pies he didn't even know were baking.

"We could have lunch tomorrow if you like." Her Cheshire Cat smile gave Max a sinking feeling that, like the fictional feline, she might do a disappearing act.

"Are you fasting until then, or can I bring you something from the deli?"

Her eyes brightened considerably at the suggestion. Hunger won out. "I'd love a tuna on rye, hold the mayo. Extra tomato and a pickle."

"Something to drink?"

"Lemonade. No dessert." She patted her tummy, then reached for her purse and pulled out a five-dollar bill.

"My treat, remember?" Max said as he exited.

A half hour later, he dragged her onto the veranda, where he'd set up a picnic lunch. Her stream of mumbled protests turned into a gasp of pleasure when she saw the red-and-white-checked table cloth, the bouquet of yellow jonquils and the loaf of French bread peeking out of a straw basket.

He might get to first base yet, Max thought as he unloaded the picnic basket. Maybe the warm spell that had hit the area was a good omen.

"Hey, I thought I said no dessert?" Jane said as Max displayed one delicacy after another.

"Potato salad is not dessert—"

"Cole slaw? Brie?"

"And your tuna, no mayo," he said, grinning back.

"A jar of pickles?"

"To go along with the quart of lemonade," Max replied, "After all, it's nearly two o'clock in the afternoon."

"I *am* hungry," she confessed, eyeing the goodies before them.

"Me, too," he echoed softly, holding her gaze.

At four o'clock, Max gave a nod of approval to the printers. *The Alexandrian* had finally stepped into the twentieth century. The new equipment along with the advertisers he had managed to drum up should enable the paper to eventually go to press seven days a week. They'd always been a local newspaper: Max liked it that way, but maybe now they'd be able to give the community more in-depth reports and a special Sunday supplement. Of course, a little more backing wouldn't hurt. Jane was right about one thing: Aries were impatient.

She really ought to see this though, he decided as he took the basement steps two at a time. Although he hadn't been able to figure out what she was up to that evening, lunch had been quite enjoyable, and it wasn't only because of the balmy weather. Jane had definitely lowered her defenses and seemed more open to Max. They had talked, just talked, although he had to admit he'd have liked a little more physical contact than simply passing the pickles.

As he reached Jane's door, he heard muffled voices coming from within. He paused to listen; Rufus and Sherry were talking excitedly to Jane.

"I'm sorry if I let the cat out of the bag to Rufus," Max heard Sherry say, "but I don't think it's fair to Max. Not after all he's done."

"Sherry's right," Rufus said. "It might be wise to cancel tonight's date."

"Max isn't going to know about it," Jane said. "I know you all mean well, but Max doesn't own me. Besides, I plan on having fun tonight."

Max slowly stepped away from the door. Normally his first inclination would have been to burst in and ask what the hell was going on, but he wasn't about to make a fool of himself. He'd read "Greta's" column that morning and he'd be darned if he'd act like a typical Aries. So, she thought all Aries rammed their way through obstacles, did she? He'd prove her wrong, if it was the last thing he did. Anyway, he'd check with Rufus later that day and get the scoop.

He was wrong. And Camilla, the society page editor, told Max that his friend left work early and she doubted if he'd be in till Monday morning. "It's spring, you know, Maxie!" She winked, and lifting her bejeweled fingers off the computer keys added, "*L'amour* is in the air!"

Turning on his heels, Max shelved his good intentions and headed down the hall to Jane's office. He'd had about enough of her artful dodging. He didn't even pause at the door, but went through it like a linebacker holding the ball.

"Max!" She looked up from the phone that was cradled on her shoulder, then putting her hand over the mouthpiece said, "It's—" her eyes clouded "—it's just a friend. But I'll be off in a jiffy. Why don't you... uh..."

"Take a cold shower?" Agitation mounted in him. He wasn't about to hang out where he wasn't wanted or listen at keyholes. She could have her damn privacy and Max's blessing on the guy on the other end of the line.

"Max, wait a minute." As she returned her attention to the phone, he heard her muttered, "Drat it all!" Then to her caller she said, "No, no. Of course I'm not upset with you. No, no—you know I'm looking forward to seeing you."

"Just a friend," was it? He'd see about that. Grabbing his jacket, Max ran out the front door and headed for the gym. He'd get in his laps, bench press and do a few hundred push-ups. By then, he'd either be thinking straight or his amnesia would have returned. In either case, he'd shower and go out for dinner.

Jane's fingers were trembling as she fastened the fancy gold loops onto her ears. Steady girl, she admonished herself, stepping back from the hall mirror to get a quick look. It was a good thing she'd dressed before going to work; as it was, she only had ten minutes to get to the Pisces Moon. She'd quickly piled her hair on top of her head, outlined her eyes and put on a dime-store red lipstick she'd picked up on the way home. The gold earrings were a last-minute idea: they had that same chunky quality as Dr. Zodiac's jewelry. She hoped he would be entranced. She also hoped she didn't blow it.

"Well, what do you guys think?" she asked her dogs as she leaned over to straighten the seam on one black-stockinged leg. They barked in approval, then charged down the hall and scooted out the dog door.

"Everything's going to be fine," Jane announced to the mirror. So what if her heels were too high, her hair too teased? So what if she felt as though she'd been assembled from papier-mâché? She was going through with it. Picking up her beaded purse and silk jacket, she headed out the door. After all, it wasn't every day she got to dress to the thrift-shop nines.

Slipping behind the wheel of her car, she wondered if Max had noticed the sixties cocktail dress she'd worn to work. Then again, how many men kept up with fashion? Of course, Max wasn't most men. That was exactly how Rufus had put it this afternoon.

Jane started Blue Gem's engine and tried not to think about Sherry's and Rufus's well-intended advice. Thank God she hadn't told them where she was meeting Dr. Zodiac. Knowing Rufus, he'd undoubtedly have wanted to station himself at the bar. Wouldn't that have been cute? Heavens, to hear them go on, one would think Dr. Z. was Jack the Ripper instead of a two-bit flim-flam man. Well, maybe not two-bit. Still, what could go wrong in public?

Ten minutes later however, as she parked in front of the Pisces Moon, she secretly wondered if what she was doing was the wisest thing. At least she had her microcassette recorder. And since it was a little late for regrets, she might as well get the story she came for and have a good time doing it.

The Pisces Moon claimed to have once been a fifties coffeehouse turned sixties hippie joint. Its most recent incarnation was as a glitzy bar. The truth was a little simpler: it had been built five years ago, and the only thing to recommend the red-brick building was the spectacular view of the Potomac River. It was about as genuine as Dr. Zodiac. The food was nouvelle cuisine, the drinks, exotic, and most of the customers were tourists in search of Old Town Alexandria atmosphere. The red-brick interior boasting gas lights seemed to fill that bill admirably for the thirsty throng that amassed there every evening.

Since it was still early and the place was, thankfully, not crowded, Jane spotted Dr. Z. immediately. He was at the circular brass bar, and from the look in his eye, more than ready for their date.

"Miss Starr, I am enchanted that once again we meet." Taking her hand, he briefly kissed it, then added, "I've gotten us a table, and took the liberty of ordering a Pink Lady for you. It seems to suit the occasion."

"My favorite," Jane enthused. He'd selected a corner table with a view of the river, and the dance floor was only a step away. The tuxedo-jacketed band members were just starting to tune up, but Dr. Z., who had reached across the table to clasp Jane's hand, seemed oblivious to this.

"I have waited centuries for this meeting," he murmured, tightening his hold on her hand, "and now, at last, we are reunited and—"

His discourse was interrupted as the waiter placed two frosty concoctions before them.

"To ecstasy," Dr. Z. said, clinking their glasses together. Then, removing the tiny parasol, he consumed half the drink in a single swallow. He smiled above the rim and said, "And to my own Pink Lady." With a wave of his hand, he motioned for another round. Jane decided he definitely believed in spirits. Especially the kind that came in bottles.

Thankfully, Jane had eaten some crackers on her way there, for her drink was a powerhouse. But if Dr. Zodiac wanted to drink, that was one way to loosen his tongue. Toward this end, Jane hung on his every word, nursed her drink and watched as he consumed three more Pink Ladies.

By the time the fourth arrived, his tongue was well-oiled. He'd already given a synopsis of several of their past lives together, and was finally coming into the twentieth century. According to his vision, he had struggled through many incarnations, and now he was reaping his rewards. He was certain he would be hailed as a genius someday.

"I can certainly see how you get your following," Jane said, running her finger around the rim of her glass. "It's amazing how easily the spirit world responds to you."

Leaning forward, in a hushed voice he confided, "I have my methods."

"I'm sure they're brilliant," she said encouragingly.

"Modern technology," he confessed, holding his drink in midair. "Since I have no doubt that the spirit exists, it doesn't bother me to sort of coax them along. Rather like in the theater or a magic show. I'm simply giving the people what they want—solace, comfort and a chance to connect with their loved ones."

"Why, how ingenious!"

"My feelings exactly. We all benefit. After all, money is merely energy, and all of my clients have reported such peace of mind after our little sessions."

"Mrs. Ritchie certainly seemed thrilled with seeing her deceased husband. How did you do it?"

"Holograms, dearest Amber. With the aid of laser beams, I was able to project his image into the room. The mist comes from a machine beneath the flooring, and an electronic device makes the séance table move.

This is nothing compared to the magic shows I used to do!''

''Oh, you were a magician. What made you change professions?''

''There's always more money to be had when you're dealing with the other side. People will pay absolute fortunes to have that little chat they neglected to have while the person was still in the body.'' His eyes glazed over slightly, then tipping his glass, he finished off the contents and waved for another. ''Ah, but you, my dear fortunately are very much in the corpus. Ah, and it is most *delecti!*''

''You're too kind,'' Jane murmured, then reaching over, she stroked his hand encouragingly. Of course, she knew that kindness had absolutely nothing to do with it, but she had to say something. She only hoped that their conversation had been successfully recorded.

Grasping her hand, he lifted it to his lips. ''To think that we've waited since our entombment for this rapture.''

''It *has* been a long time,'' Jane remarked, trying gracefully to retrieve her hand.

''But now we can be united forever.'' His eyes, like shiny daggers, met hers.

''Right.'' She gave a tug on her hand. Furtively she looked around for some possible diversion.

''We have a date with destiny,'' Dr. Z. purred, ''and this time we mustn't be late.''

''But the moon is void of course,'' Jane protested.

''We are beyond all that.''

I'll say we are, she thought, feeling decidedly uncomfortable.

When Max entered the Pisces Moon, he was looking for an escape from his own thoughts. He'd been driving along the river when the idea of an ice-cold beer had drawn him into the bar. He hadn't been there five minutes before he spotted her.

At first, he couldn't believe his eyes, but he knew right away it was Jane. And from the cozy look of things, she and her "friend" were having quite a fine time. Still, Max was a little surprised that she'd go for that type, not that he could see that much of the man in the dim light, but what he saw was enough. Jane was practically in the guy's lap.

What was it that blasted horoscope had said this morning? Something about Aries watching their tempers? What temper? he thought, as he pushed away from the bar.

Slowly, he crossed the room, beer in hand. He was in control, he assured himself. He could have overturned tables, but he didn't. He merely went slightly bonkers.

He stood over Jane and poured his beer onto her lap. Max had never done anything like that before. It was something he'd seen done in old movies, the kind of thing Cary Grant would do to Katherine Hepburn.

Jane had seen him coming, seen the look on his face, and had known exactly what he was thinking, though she hadn't expected a shower. Somehow this oddly endearing display showed Max really cared, and it certainly solved her dilemma with Dr. Z.

"Maxwell!" she cried, jumping to her feet, "this *is* a surprise. When did you get into town?" Latching onto him, she skirted introductions and on the pretense of getting more drinks, hastily steered Max around the bar and out the door.

"What the devil—"

"I don't have time to explain," Jane said, glancing back into the bar. Dr. Z. was still seated at their table.

"Your problem is you never have time to explain. Sometimes I think you're in a different time zone than the rest of the world."

"Max, that's not fair. Besides, I will explain. You'll see. But," she added perkily as she stepped around to her car, "since I'm not going to ask why you dumped your beer on me, you ought to give me the benefit of the doubt, too." With a smile, she ducked into the car.

"Just try me! I'd love to tell you why." He was holding on to her car door as if he were going to hitch a ride.

"Tomorrow, Maxwell." She gunned the engine.

"Janey, tomorrow never comes for you! How about right now?"

"How 'bout later?"

"I want to know what you were doing out with a—a used-car salesman!"

"What's wrong with used-car salesmen? Someone has to do it." Max was jealous, she thought as a delicious and unexpected warmth shot through her. Still, this was not the time or place for passionate declarations.

"Of course, someone has to do it. But you told me—"

"A little fib, I know. But that was earlier."

"But why? And what were you doing with him in there in the first place? And don't tell me it had to do with the stars or I'll—"

"But it did."

"Right. I suppose you were interviewing him for your book."

"Max, I've got to go! See you first thing in the morning."

"You're not going anywhere till you tell me what you and that man were doing."

"Oh, very well! We were about to make passionate love. Satisfied? But please, don't think your timely appearance wasn't appreciated—"

"Do you usually walk out on dates?"

"Depends on the date," she replied sweetly. "I'd never walk out on you."

"Your batting average proves you wrong."

"I've striving to improve that. How about I give you a lift somewhere?"

"My car's across the street, thanks just the same."

An odd look flitted across his face as he let go of the door, then without glancing back, crossed to his car. Jane suddenly wanted to call him back. Didn't he know she was teasing him? Tomorrow she'd explain the whole thing to him, and then ... Then what?

Sure, Max had been jealous, but that just went with the Aries territory. It didn't mean he felt all the things she was feeling. And for the first time in her life, Jane knew what she was feeling. Putting the car into gear, she pulled away from the curb and headed in the opposite direction from where Max was going. Thankfully, Dr. Zodiac had remained in the bar, awaiting her return.

Jane could hardly wait to get home; she had all the proof she needed. She'd done the job, and if necessary, she'd stay up all night writing the story. Nothing could stop her now.

Three hours later, she let out a sigh, then pushing away from her desk, took a gulp of her now-cold coffee while her printer spewed out the story. If she had a fax machine, she would have sent the article straight to the office. However, she planned on getting to work early and would have the entire package, including séance photos, on Max's desk before he arrived. So why wasn't she excited? Considering everything she'd been through, she should have been on cloud nine. So why was she so depressed?

She stood up and stretched; that helped some. Maybe she was suffering postcreative letdown? No, that wasn't it. It wasn't the stars, either. It was Max. Plain and simple. She'd wanted to show him what a clever, industrious, independent woman she was, and she had succeeded. Boy, had she ever!

Jane glanced at the last page of the article as it rolled out of the printer: it was good. Page-one material. And Max would like it; but there was something else she wanted from him, only now she doubted if it would be so freely offered.

She wanted Max. She loved Max, God bless him. She was even willing to risk her precious independence for him. And what had she done earlier? Thanked him for rescuing her from Dr. Z.? No. She'd teased him about their love-making. Someday, surely, she'd learn to think before she spoke.

Jane was the first to arrive at the office the following morning. She had a quick cup of coffee while she jotted Max a note. She tore up the note, wrote a second one and shredded it, too. Finally she decided to just put the story on his desk. On impulse, she snatched up *The Mystery of Larkspur Lane* to use as a paperweight, then headed down the hall to Max's office. The place was still fairly quiet except for the buzz of voices coming from the kitchen area.

She rapped softly on Max's door. No one answered. Quietly she entered and crossed the room. Carefully she placed the story and photos in the center of the desk. She was about to put the Nancy Drew book on top when Max entered. He looked as though he'd been wrung through the printing press, if that were possible. His jeans were too snug to be rumpled, but the rest of him definitely needed tending to. The fact that he had a tie in one hand and an electric razor in the other was a hopeful sign; the five o'clock shadow though, only added to his haggard expression. She must have been staring at him, for with a laugh, he spun the tie in the air and crossing over to her said, "Don't worry, I'm not about to hang myself."

"I wasn't thinking you were, though you do look a bit—"

"Worse for wear?" He moved closer and she could smell shampoo and after-shave. Damp, blond curls clung to his forehead, and she felt an irrational longing to brush them to one side.

"I'm sorry about last night," Jane said after an interminable pause, "but I've got something to show you."

"Nancy Drew?" he asked, indicating the book she was waving under his nose. "You found a first edition or something?" He plucked it from her, then with a slow smile said, "This is the same old Larkspur Lane."

"No, there's something else. C'mon over here." Pointing to the story she added, "This is to make up for last night."

"Oh? And it's perfectly okay for me to go dumping drinks on you?" Leisurely he picked up the story.

"At least it wasn't a Pink Lady."

"Next thing you'll be blaming my Aries sun."

"Well, they *are* quick-tempered," she allowed.

"I've been doing a little reading up on them," he confessed, leaning one hip on the edge of his desk, "And it would appear we're a hot-headed, self-centered, impatient and jealous lot." Tearing open the envelope, he murmured, "We like to think we set the world and everything in it on fire."

"Don't forget they're courageous and . . . and—"

"Charming?" he suggested as he pulled her copy out of the envelope. "You know, I've been wondering if you might do my chart. Oh, not that I believe it."

" 'Tommy rot,' is what you called it."

"I've said and done a lot of things since meeting you." With a laugh he added, "I just didn't have such an obliging sounding board before."

"You do surprise me," Jane conceded, wondering where all this was leading.

"Let's say we surprise each other. And last night was sort of the icing on the cake. Although I can't really blame you for going out with that used-car salesman—"

"Wait a minute!" Jane exclaimed, "that used-car salesman happened to be Dr. Zodiac, and I—"

"Dr. Z.?"

"Yep. Astroscope's Dr. Zodiac."

"Hey, I thought we had an agreement—"

"You had the agreement. I was simply being agreeable. Now if you'll cool down and take a look at my article and the photo of Dr. Z, you'll see I've taken no risks at all. Well, none to speak of. . . ."

Max's eyes snapped up from the photo to meet hers. "Except for that bozo pawing you last night."

"Granted, a low point. But you saved the day by spilling your drink on me. Not that he would have actually done anything. Still, he was fairly intent on reliving some pretty torrid past lives.''

"Damn!" Max flashed Jane a menacing look and was about to add something else, but instead slapped the photo and article back onto his desk. "Did anyone ever tell you that you are the most exasperating woman on the face of the planet?"

"Pops did. By the way, he's coming down to cover a story." Jane bit back a smile. "Might as well tell you— he wants to do a report on *The Alexandrian*. Hope you don't mind." With a nod toward the unread article, she added, "Let me know what changes you'd like. Maybe we can discuss them over dinner tonight. That is, if you're still free."

"If *I'm* still..." His hand snaked out. Drawing her toward him he said, "On second thought, I will be pretty busy. You see, I've got this new employee I've got to keep in line. I've tried about everything I can think of except the last resort." Slowly, he cupped her face with his hands and looking steadily into her eyes he said, "We had a rocky beginning—"

"Oh?" Jane's heart was thumping like mad and she was having difficulty breathing.

"Very rough. I fired her sight unseen. Guess I thought she was a kook." Gently, his thumbs caressed her cheeks, and his lips brushed every so slightly against hers.

"And was she...a kook?" Jane murmured the question against his mouth.

"Umm-hmm. A delicious kook, who—"

A loud knock sounded at Max's door, followed by, "Yo! Chief— Oops... Catch you later." Doffing his Redskins cap, the sports writer backed out of the office.

"Where was I?" Max asked, tightening his hold on Jane.

"Don't you remember?" Jane asked breathlessly.

"Blame it on my amnesia. It's sort of like malaria—it reoccurs."

"Oh, it does, does it?"

"Some things I remember real well, though," he whispered in her ear. Then drawing back, he gazed intently at her, and the hunger in his eyes made Jane weak with pleasure. "Like the feel of a certain woman in my arms, soft and silky, sassy and sweet. And a little frightened."

She blinked in surprise, "You don't miss much."

"Remember, I was once an investigative reporter." Smoothing back a lock of her hair he added, "Between the two of us, I'd say we make a fair team."

"You haven't read my article on Dr. Z. yet."

"In good time. First things first. Besides, you're Randolph Smith's daughter...." He paused to nibble her earlobe, then said, "So, Pops is coming down here just in time. I take it that was the friend you were talking with on the phone yesterday."

"Yes, but what do you mean 'just in time'?" Straightening, she looked at Max carefully. "Are you keeping something from me?"

"Hey, that's my line." As he pulled her back into his arms, the door opened once again, this time admitting the culinary editor.

"Let me guess," Max said, "you want to know what we're cooking up, right? Well, it's a wedding cake!"

"A wedding cake?" Jane's heart threw in an extra beat, but Max merely crooked his arm around her neck and playfully drew her against his chest.

"Three tiers," Max announced, "so I suppose you might as well invite the entire staff in. Ah, here's Rufus now. He can be best man."

"Max—"

"Well, you *are* going to marry me, aren't you?"

"We've—we've never even discussed it..." An odd wave of dizziness passed over Jane. He'd actually asked her! "I—I have to think."

"We do too much of that as it is." Then looking up at the others in the room he said, "Guess you'd better send in Camilla so she can write the official announcement of our engagement."

"Max, I haven't said yes yet." Jane grinned up at him. Then, grasping his shirt collar, she drew him closer. "But I suppose you need someone to remind you who you are. And I guess I could use someone to sort of keep track of me."

"I had other things in mind," he murmured against her lips as he waved their audience away.

"Oh? Like what?" But his kiss, deep and full, drove all thoughts from her.

"That, for starters," he replied when his lips finally left hers. Then gazing into her amethyst eyes, he knew her fearful doubts were gone. And the love that shone from them was brighter than any star he'd ever seen.

"That was quite a kiss," she said at length, drumming her fingers against his chest.

"Will you marry me? Or do I have to hold you prisoner all day?"

"Umm, what an interesting proposal." She flashed him a smile. "And you'd really do it, wouldn't you?"

"Yep. Might not hold you down with a German shepherd, but I'd find ways to keep you occupied." His hands slowly skimmed the length of her, settled on her hips, then pulled her abruptly against him. He reveled in the sigh this elicited.

"Well, I suppose if we're ever to get any work done, I'd better say yes."

Max felt her trembled response, then cupping her chin, tilted it so she had to look at him.

"Give me another reason for saying yes," he demanded.

Lord, Max almost knew her better than she knew herself. All along he'd understood her fears of being too vulnerable, and he'd waited with a patience she'd rarely seen in a man and never in an Aries! But the waiting was over; he'd humored her long enough.

"Yes!" she blurted through sudden tears. "And the only reason I can think of is that somewhere along the line, I fell in love with you."

"That's about the best reason I can think of," Max murmured, gently caressing her face. "I can't remember not loving you. It's only been a week, but it feels like forever." Dropping a kiss on her lips, he added, "I guess we ought to just thank our lucky stars."

"Oh good heavens, that reminds me, I've got to get my column done. And Sherry left a message about meeting for lunch—it probably has to do with Rufus."

"They'll work things out," Max said softly. "If we did, anyone can."

"Oh." Jane took a breath. "Well . . . I guess I don't have to really do anything, do I?"

With a laugh, Max pulled her back into his arms. "That's right. For now, why don't we let the world revolve on its own. It'll still be here when we get back."

"Back?" Her eyes were sparkling with anticipation.

"Yes, from our honeymoon. That is, after Pops gets here and we get married."

"Honeymoon?"

"I love you when you're excited—"

"Max, we have to make plans . . ." Her eyes widened. "You do?"

"You bet."

"Oh, Max . . ." Surrendering her lips to his, all thoughts abandoned her. All but one: Max loved her as much as she loved him, and would go on loving her for as long as there were stars to count in the heavens.

MORE ABOUT
THE ARIES MAN

by Lydia Lee

Aries men are bursting with creative energy, courage and a childlike belief that they can do anything they start out to do in half the time it takes other mortals to do it, *and* that they'll come out *numero uno*. After all, their planetary ruler is Mars, the ancient god of war and action. And speaking of action, Aries men have two speeds: park and fourth gear. You see, the Aries man's life is an open book, and he's about as uncomplicated as they come. Like his symbol, the ram, his approach to life is direct, and whatever is in his path he'll sweep aside. He's the first of the three fire signs—the other two are Leo and Sagittarius—and as such, he shares their exuberance and enthusiasm. His major weakness is probably his naiveté coupled with self-centeredness. It's nothing personal, mind you, but like a child, he simply sees himself as first. Don't forget, he *is* the first sign of the zodiac, and if you want to tie for first place in his life, you'd better make him first in yours.

Now that we've bared his Big Flaw, let's go on to extoll his numerous virtues: there's not a mean bone in his body, he's got enough courage for ten men, he's generous, gives sincere compliments and is faithful, once he decides you're his lady. His direct approach to passion positively sizzles. But let *him* approach you. Remember the *numero uno* rule: nothing will wilt his legendary fervor faster than the brass-knuckles approach of a fanatical feminist. Whatever you do, don't declare your undying feelings first. However, once he's won you and you're involved in a committed relationship, don't be too cool. Let him know you care, but don't smother him, or he might seek greener pastures. A little mystery will keep his interest, though too much will make him go crazy. If he suspects you're seeing another man, there will definitely be a scene. Aries is the jealous type!

That brings us to something else you'd better know about the ram: he's got a straw-fire temper, and when something is bothering him, he'll let it out—*fast!* Then he'll forget about it so quickly, your head will spin. If these pyrotechnics are too much, you might want to consider linking up with a calm, steady Taurus. However, before you change partners and dance off into the sunset, you should consider the flip side of this coin: more than any other sign, with the exception of Scorpio, the Aries male is very much in touch with his animal nature. Although he may be naive in some ways, he doesn't carry around a lot of emotional baggage. The man has a happy knack for forgetting failures, broken marriages and other troubles that litter life's path.

If you're lucky enough to have captured this ram's heart, you might just be one of those rare couples who keep the fires burning brighter with each succeeding anniversary. But where can you meet one of these fearless, ardent lovers? A fireman's ball for starters, a Smithsonian expedition to Kenya, or the Indianapolis 500. Then again, he might just be the man next door, and won't you be the lucky one!

*   *   *   *   *

Famous Aries Men

Gregory Peck
Warren Beatty
Omar Sharif
Arturo Toscanini
Thomas Jefferson

Take 4 bestselling love stories FREE

Plus get a FREE surprise gift!

IT'S A CELEBRATION OF MOTHERHOOD!

Following the success of BIRDS, BEES and BABIES, we are proud to announce our second collection of Mother's Day stories.

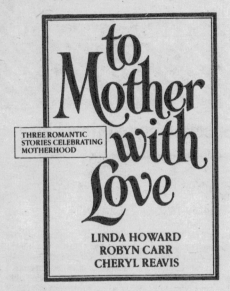

to **Mother** *with* **Love**

THREE ROMANTIC
STORIES CELEBRATING
MOTHERHOOD

**LINDA HOWARD
ROBYN CARR
CHERYL REAVIS**

Three stories in one volume, all by award-winning authors—stories especially selected to reflect the love all families share.

Available in May, TO MOTHER WITH LOVE is a perfect gift for yourself or a loved one to celebrate the joy of motherhood.

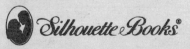

Silhouette Books®

ML-1